THE LONG WALK

A RITE OF PASSAGE STORY

MILTON J DAVIS

MVmedia, LLC
Fayetteville, GA

Milton J. Davis/MVmedia, LLC
PO Box 1465
Fayetteville, GA 30214
www.mvmediaatl.com
www.miltonjdavis.com

Publisher's Note: This is a work of fiction. Names, characters, places, and incidents are a product of the author's imagination. Locales and public names are sometimes used for atmospheric purposes. Any resemblance to actual people, living or dead, or to businesses, companies, events, institutions, or locales is completely coincidental.

Book Layout ©2017BookDesignTemplates.com
Cover Art by Sean Hill

Ordering Information:
Quantity sales. Special discounts are available on quantity purchases by corporations, associations, and others. For details, contact the "Special Sales Department" at the address above.

The Long Walk/Milton J. Davis. -- 1st ed.
ISBN No. 978-1-7372277-7-9

Contents

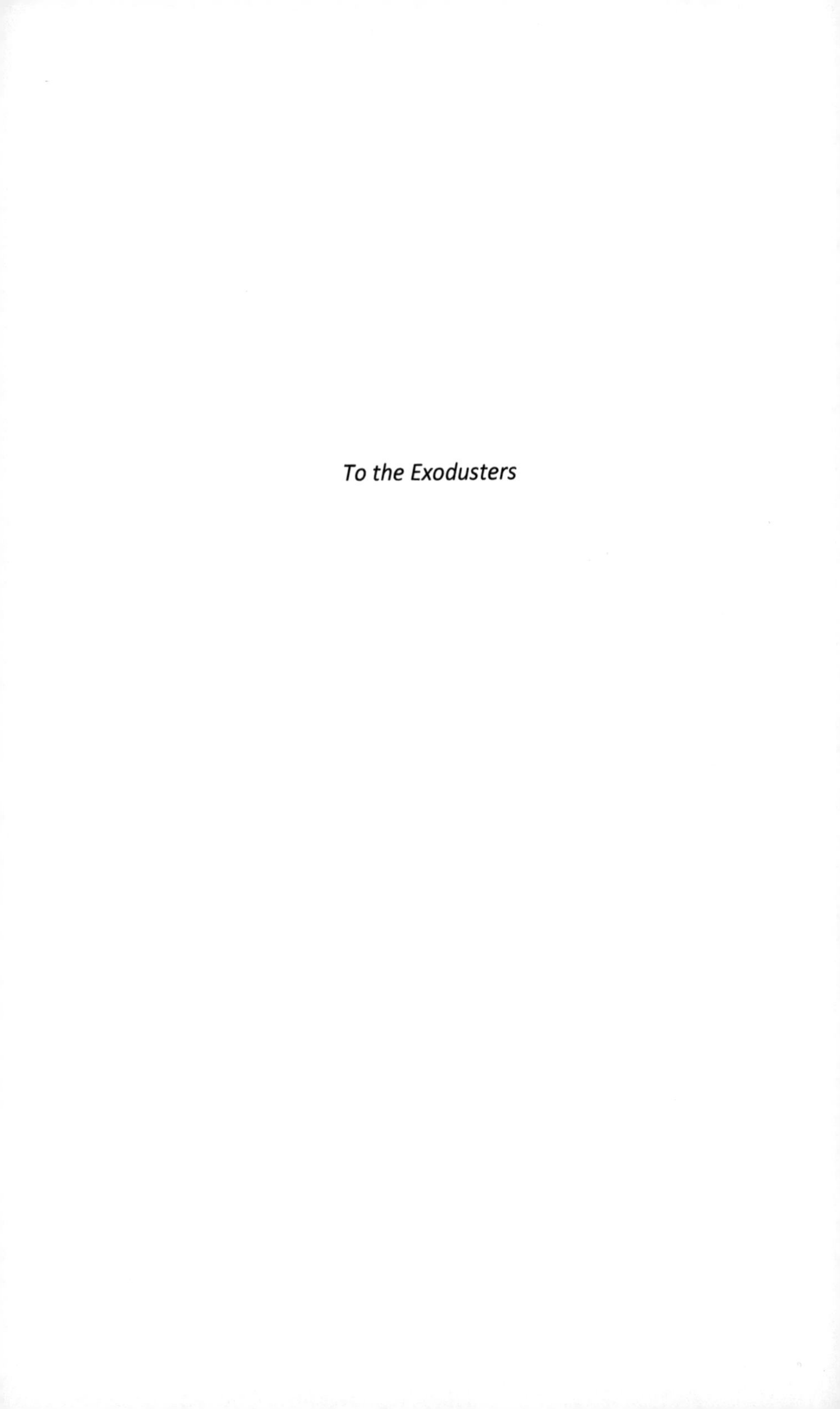

To the Exodusters

ONE

Patience de Verteuil made the sign of the cross as the steamship *Steebeth* pulled away from Invaders Bay. She was leaving Trinidad behind, setting out on an unexpected journey sparked by a letter her father received from an old friend, Harriet Tubman. She looked up to her father standing beside her, searching his strong brown face for any signs of doubt but there were none. They were on their way to America, to a city she never heard of until a few weeks ago; Nicodemus.

She tugged at her father's white cotton shirt and he looked at her with smiling eyes.

"What is it, *cheri*?" he asked.

"Are you sure about this, papa?"

He squatted before her then hugged her with his thick arms. Papa was a big man, dwarfing her despite the growth spurt that came with her twelfth birthday. Other things had come as well, things that papa had a hard time explaining to her. He took her instead to Sister Rosa. She wished mama could have told her such things, but mama had died so long ago, Patience barely remembered her. There was a painting of her in their old house that Patience would stare at and imagine them having conversations about flowers, food and sometimes boys. The thought made her smile as papa hugged her.

"I'm sure," he said. "Miss Tubman would not have sent for me if it wasn't necessary."

"Is she so important that we must leave our home?"

Papa nodded. "Miss Tubman is a very special person. She has a great responsibility that she cannot bear alone. I and others must assist her."

"Are the others from Trinidad, too?"

"No. They live in America. You will meet them when we arrive at Nicodemus, if not before."

"Do they have children?"

He swept Patience into his arms then sat her on the bulwark.

"My little bird is always chirping! Your questions will be answered soon enough. But now we'll wave goodbye to our island and our friends!"

Patience waved with papa, but she could not act as if she was happy. She hoped whatever papa had to do for this Miss Tubman would be over soon and they could return home. The wind tugged at her bonnet so she waved with one hand.

"I'll be home soon," she whispered. "Very soon."

They lingered on the deck until nightfall. There were very few children on the ship and all of those were white. Patience had no issue playing with them, but their parents wouldn't allow it. She stayed close to papa instead, gazing out onto the waters. As an island girl the beach and the ocean were a daily part of her life, but never had she been so far out to sea that she could not see land. She felt so small in the midst of the ocean, so she clung to papa to feel important.

They took their supper and dinner on the deck. The Negro rooms on the steamer were near the steam engine, making them cramped, loud and hot. Papa did his best to get a better cabin but the white men on this ship weren't nice like the ones sailing between the islands. At least the severs were Negroes as well. They brought them ham, potatoes and sweet tea.

Night arrived and the deck hands walked the deck, lighting the gas lamps for those enjoying the cool air. The excitement and apprehension of a new journey had worn away. Patience was restless.

"Papa,' she said sweetly. "Can we play?"

Papa frowned. "This isn't the place," he replied. "They don't know anything about bois. Somebody might think I'm trying to give you a whupping."

Patience giggled. "Just a little bit, papa. Please?"

Papa thought for a moment, tapping his fingers on his chin.

"Okay, this one time," he finally said. "Let's go."

They fast walked to the cabin, the engine's voice louder the closer they came to their room. It was almost deafening as they entered. At least whoever built this ship knew this would be a loud area and took the care to make the little cabin soundproof, at least soundproof enough to allow sleep. Papa reached under the bed then extracted a long narrow box covered in rich leather and accented with golden studs. Patience's eyes widened with curiosity. She'd never see it before.

"What's that, papa?"

Papa shoved it back under the bed.

"Wrong box." He reached under the bed again then pulled out the old battered box containing their bois.

"Here we are," he announced.

"Papa, what was in that other box?" Patience asked as they left the room.

"Nothing, just some old things from home," he answered.

She followed papa out of the room then through the hallway.

"I've never seen it before," she said.

"I hope you haven't," papa replied. "That would mean you've been going through my things and I know you know better than that."

He turned and gave Patience a serious stare.

"No papa, I haven't gone through your things," she said, answering his expression.

He smiled. "Good. Now let's play."

They emerged onto the deck then went to the stern. Papa opened the box then handed Patience her bois, a thin stick painted red and green. Papa took out his bois and Patience covered her mouth to muffle her giggle. Papa's stick was a poor looking thing, but she knew its sting well. So did many of the other players in her town.

Papa grasped his stick on both ends then raised it to the guard position. Patience did the same. They began to step in time before Papa began to sing, his rich baritone filling the night air.

Mooma, Mooma
Your son in de grave already,
Your son in de grave already,
Take a towel and ban you belly,
Mooma, Mooma,
Today is your son's burial,
Today is your r son's burial,
Tomorrow is a grand funeral...

Papa slid his hands together at the stick's base then struck down on her slowly, setting the pace. They exchanged blows as they danced in time. Patience joined her father singing in harmony, her falsetto voice light and playful.

Mooma, Mooma,

Your son in de grave already,
Your son in de grave already,
Take a towel and ban your belly.
Mooma, Mooma,
Today is the grand funeral,
Today is the grand funeral,
Next time it's the grand burial!

"What the hell is this?"

Two white men dressed in tailored suits emerged into their light. One was a tall, ruddy man wearing a bowler and smoking a pipe, the other somewhat shorter and wider. Papa looked at Patience and she quickly came to his side. There was something odd about the two, something threatening. It took Patience a few moments to figure it out. It was their eyes. They reflected the light like the eyes of cats.

"They were doing some kind of dancing thing with those sticks," the tall man said.

"You know how they are," the shorter man said. "Always dancing and singing about something."

The tall man took his pipe out then pointed at Papa. "Y'all go on ahead now. We need some entertainment on this tub."

"We were just finishing, sir," Papa said.

"You heard the man!" the shorter man barked.

"Now, now Jim, this ain't Mississippi," the man said. "These niggers here ain't used to our ways. Listen how they're talking. Y'all from Jamaica?"

"Trinidad, sir," Papa replied. Patience heard the anger in papa's voice.

The tall man walked up to Patience then grasped her bois. She began to pull away but Papa shook his head. She let it go.

The man examined the stick, holding it like a fencing sword. He looked at Papa with a sly grin.

"Let's give it a go," he said.

Papa nodded. The man took a formal fencing stance; Papa gripped his bois, hands on the opposite ends. The man began prancing about then stopped.

"No, this ain't right," the man said. He looked at Patience.

"Gal, sing that little song."

Patience looked at Papa for permission and he nodded. Why was he being so nice to these people? she thought.

She sang. The man hopped about, poking at Papa while Papa blocked. She was shocked when Papa actually let the man prod him once or twice, but then she saw the frustration building in his face. He nodded at her and she grinned. She sang faster.

"This is fun!" the tall man exclaimed.

Papa moved close to the tall man then pretended to stumble. His hands slid together and he swung hard. The tall man was quick, raising Patience's bois to block Papa blow. But Papa's bois smashed against her bois, driving it into the tall man's head. Both sticks cracked against the man's forehead. The tall man's eyes went wide then closed as he collapsed to the deck.

"Mr. Jenkins!"

Jim reached the tall man just as he collapsed onto the deck.

Papa knelt beside Jim; his face filled with mock concern. Patience covered her mouth with her hand, holding back the laugh that threatened to burst free.

"I'm so sorry," Papa said. "Sometimes my feet get tied up. You should take him to the infirmary. They can take care of him."

"That won't be necessary," Jim replied. "Help me pick him up."

Papa and Jim lifted Mr. Jenkins to a sitting position then Jim maneuvered the man onto his shoulder. The stout man was stronger than he looked, walking away with his unconscious friend with ease. He turned then glared at Papa.

"You better watch yourself, boy," he snarled. "Because I will."

Papa smiled then raised his stick.

"Goodbye . . . Jim," he said. "I hope Mr. Jenkins is okay."

Patience waited until the two men were far away before dropping her hand then squealing with laughter. Papa chuckled then held his finger to his lips.

"You should have done that sooner," Patience said.

Papa shook his head. "I'm a bad example for you. This might cause us trouble."

He picked up her bois then handed it to her.

"Listen, Patience. Things will be different in America," he said. "Whites and Negroes are not as friendly to each other as they are in Trinidad. Many whites act as if Negroes are still slaves. They expect us to give way to them."

"Then we will hit them with our bois!" Patience said.

"No, we won't," Papa said. "Once we get to Nicodemus, we can let down our guard. Until then we will have to be careful. Do you understand?"

"I understand."

"Good. Now let's go to the cabin and get some sleep."

Patience smiled as Papa placed his arm around her as they strolled to the lower deck entrance. Though they traveled to a new country, she felt safe. Papa would never let anything happen to her.

She woke the next day to a clear sky and pleasant breeze. After a quick breakfast she followed Papa onto the deck with books and pencils under her arms.

"Papa, why do I have to study? Can't we wait until we're in America?"

Papa frowned at her. "And what would you rather do?"

"Sleep and practice with my bois!" she said.

Papa held up her math book. "This is stronger than any bois. An educated mind is the best weapon. The first thing I'll do when we get to Nicodemus is enroll you in school. There are black colleges in America where you can earn a degree then return to Trinidad to help our people."

Papa was always thinking ahead, but at that moment Patience wasn't interested in helping her people. She wanted to play.

"Let's play, papa," she said.

Papa frowned. "Again?"

Patience nodded.

"When you're done with your studies," he said.

Patience face drooped. "Okay."

Days strolled by, Patience and Papa occupying themselves with lessons and bois practice. Despite his best efforts Patience became bored. She took to exploring the steamship during their breaks, at least the places where she was allowed. The white people could go anywhere on the ship at any time; the black people were restricted to certain decks and only allowed on the top deck when the white people decided to leave. If America was anything like the ship, she would hate it. She hoped whatever Papa had to do for Miss Tubman didn't last long. The sooner they returned to Trinidad, the better.

It was night, the black sky peppered with a million stars. A cool breeze blew across the low undulating waves, adding crispness to the air. Patience played on deck near the stern, swinging her bois at imaginary opponents while humming.

"Where your daddy at, gal?"

Patience turned to see one of the men her father beat a week ago. The man strode toward her, a nefarious grin on his face and his eyes burning like the deck gas lamps. Terror overwhelmed her; she tucked her bois under her arm then fled for their cabin.

"Papa! Papa! That man is coming to get you!"

Patience grabbed the door handle then snatched the door open. A blast of hot air struck her and knocked her to the floor. She looked into the room and saw a sight that seemed from Hell. The room blazed, the fire consuming everything inside. In the center of the fire stood Papa, fighting savagely against a creature that seemed made of flames.

"Papa!"

Patience tried to enter the room but a hand grabbed her then dragged her away.

"Come here gal," the white man said. "Your daddy's done for!"

Patience whacked the man across the shins with her bois. He fell on his back howling.

"Damn pickaninny!"

Patience spun around. Papa's clothes burned, but he fought the creature as if he felt no pain. He ducked a swipe of the foul being's clawed hand then smacked it in the stomach with his bois. He then performed a move Patience had never seen. Papa whirled around, striking the creature across the neck. Patience screamed as the creature's head flew into the air then fell into the fire. Papa turned toward her then stumbled out of the flames. He fell out of the room onto his knees before her. Smoke wafted from his charred clothes and skin. He managed to smile through his obvious pain as he handed her his special box.

"Give this to Miss Harriet," he said. "Tell her I said he's closer than we thought."

Patience took the box then dropped it. She grabbed at Papa's hand but he jerked away.

"No baby girl," he said. "I have to finish this, or a lot of people are going to die."

He struggled to his feet then leaned over and kissed her forehead.

"I love you, Patience. I'll always be with you. As long as you have this, you'll have me."

He patted the bois box. A strange howl came from the inferno. Papa's smile faded. He raised his bois, turned, then jumped back into the flames.

"No! Papa! No!"

The white man grabbed her again. This time she let him drag her away, her eyes locked on Papa as he fought the burning apparitions. The man stopped dragging her.

"The fire's down there!" he shouted.

A score of men with water buckets rushed by them. The man continued dragging her until they reached the ship's bow where the other passengers gathered. Women and children swarmed to the life boats, the captain and the crew attempting to keep order as much as possible while loading the boats then lowered into the sea. The man scooped Patience up into his arms then headed for the nearest boat. A stern crewman stopped him before he could climb aboard.

"Women and children first," he said.

"Can't you see I have a child?" the man replied.

"Put the child in the boat with the others," the crewman said. "You wait your turn."

"She'll be lost without me!" the man said.

The crewman took a billy club from his belt.

"Put the girl in the boat then step back," he ordered.

An elderly white woman clothed in an evening gown climbed from the boat.

"I'll take her," she said. "What's her name?"

The man's face turned red.

"I thought so," the crewman said. "Get away from this boat!"

He jabbed his club in the man's chest, pushing him away.

The elderly woman cradled Patience as she climbed back into the boat.

"What's your name, gal?" she asked.

Patience didn't reply. Her voice was taken away by her last vision of her father, the flames consuming him as the apparitions shuddered from his bois blows. Papa was dead. She knew it in her heart. She closed her eyes and hoped never to open them again.

TWO

When Patience opened her eyes, she was on the deck of another ship. The elderly white woman still cradled her in her thin arms. They sat on a blanket with the other survivors. This ship had the strong odor of fish about it, making Patience's nose crinkle. No sooner did she revived did images of Papa's death overwhelm her.

"Papa," she whispered as she cried.

"There, there," the woman said. "Things will work out. Once we get to Savannah, we'll get you with your family."

"I don't have family in Savannah," Patience said. "Papa was my family."

"Oh my," the woman said. "That complicates things. What's your name?"

"Patience," she said. "Patience du Verteuil."

"What type of name is that for a Negro?" the woman asked.

"It's my name," Patience replied. "It a good name for a Negro."

The woman patted her head. "Don't mind me, girl. I'm an old woman."

"What's your name, ma'am?" Patience asked.

"Elizabeth Johnson," the woman said. Patience noticed the woman looking at the box she clutched.

"What's this?" she asked.

"It's Papa's bois," she said. "He gave it to me before . . . before . . ."

Elizabeth shared a sympathetic smile. "You hold onto that, baby. You hold on to that tight."

The woman stood, lifting Patience to her feet.

"Are you hungry?" she asked.

Patience nodded. "Yes ma'am."

"Come on. Let's get something to eat."

Elizabeth and Patience worked their way through the crowded deck to the food line. The cook shoveled out bowls of seafood chowder to the passengers. He frowned when he looked at Patience.

"We don't . . ."

"Save me your attitude," Elizabeth said. "We're hungry and you'll fix us two bowls. Otherwise I'll have some harsh words for your captain about you."

The cook scowled as he made a bowl for each of them. Patience and Miss Elizabeth returned to their space on the deck and ate their stew. It was bland yet filling. The food did little for Patience's energy. She slept as soon as she finished her bowl, dreaming of Papa and the mother she never knew. Her mind remained blank the entire journey to Savannah harbor.

Local authorities and worried relatives met the ship at the Savannah docks. The passengers dispersed among their loved ones as they disembarked, sharing stories of that terrible day. Patience looked at the strange land, the people rushing about and her depression deepened.

"I want to go home," she said. "I want to go back to Trinidad."

Miss Elizabeth squeezed her tight. "That's not going to be possible. I'll keep you with me for a time until we can find a nice Negro family to take you in."

Patience pushed away from Miss Elizabeth.

"I don't want another family!" she screamed. "I want to go home!"

She ran across the deck then down the gangplank.

"Patience! Patience!" Miss Elizabeth shouted.

Patience ignored her as she pushed through the crowd, clutching Papa's bois box tight to her chest, tears streaming down her face. Someone gripped her shoulder, stopping her in her tracks.

"Hold on there, girl," a deep voice spoke. "You gonna git yourself hurt running like that."

Patience turned about then looked up into the gentle face of a massive ebony skinned man. Something about his expression told her that this man meant her no harm. He felt familiar even though she was encountering him for the first time.

"I saw you run off that boat," he said. "I'm Big Jim. I was waiting on you and your daddy. Where is he?"

Tears welled in Patience's eyes. "He's dead."

Big Jim's smile disappeared. "What happened?"

Patience shut her eyes. "A white man was chasing me. I ran to our cabin, but when I got there, the whole room was on fire and papa was fighting some kind of things."

"Lord Jesus," Big Jim said. "They at it already."

He knelt before Patience and smiled again.

"Come on with me. Missy will get you fed and you can rest."

"I want to go home," Patience said. "I want to go back to Trinidad!"

"I'm about to tell you something you ain't gonna like," Big Jim replied. "Your home ain't safe for you no more. Them haints that got your daddy is most likely looking for you. The place where y'all were headed is the only safe place for you now. Your daddy knew it, which is why he brought you here. We'll take care of you until the others arrive then you'll have to move on as soon as you can."

"Others?"

"Yeah. You ain't the only one Miss Harriet done called for."

Big Jim stood then held her hand.

"Let's go. Missy is waiting for us."

Patience let the hulking man lead her to a wagon hitched to two white mules. She climbed into the wagon, clutching Papa's box under her arm. They rode through Savannah, the mules' hooves clacking against the cobblestone streets. Patience barely noticing the old buildings and majestic live oaks that made Savannah a jewel in many folks' eyes. Soon they traversed a sandy dirt road bordered by patches of marsh, live oaks and tea colored tidal creeks. Patience was tired but she could not sleep. Her world was suddenly gone, her future dark as a moonless night. She looked at the man who called himself Big Jim then cleared her throat.

"Mr. Jim, where are you taking me?"

Big Jim looked at her and smiled.

"It ain't Mr. Jim, just Big Jim. Some grown folks don't like children talking to them unless they're respectful but I don't care either way. Like I said before, I'm taking you to Missy."

"Is Miss Missy a witch?"

Big Jim laughed. "Some folks would call her that, but them folks don't understand what she do."

"What is she, then?" Patience asked.

"She's a priestess," Big Jim answered.

"Can she . . . can she kill those things that killed Papa?"

"No," Big Jim said. "All she can do is get you ready for the journey ahead. Now them folks you'll be traveling with? They something else."

"Who are they?"

Big Jim smiled. "You'll find out when the time comes."

Dusk settled across the marsh as they reached Missy's house, a wide white-washed building surrounded by moss draped live oaks. The canopies of the ancient trees meshed over the house in a leafy crown that blocked the sun from every direction. A brown and black hound dog lounged on the steps leading to the front porch; its ears raised then the dog jumped to its paws. It let out a long howl before barking.

"Be quiet, Beau!" Big Jim shouted. "Ain't nobody but me!"

The screen door to the house screeched open and Missy stepped out onto the porch. She was a tall woman, just as tall as Big Jim, heavy-set with ebony skin, light brown eyes and a generous smile.

"That you, Jim?" she shouted.

"Yes ma'am!" Jim shouted back.

Missy wiped her hands on her flower patterned apron as she ambled to the edge of the porch.

"Who that you got with you? You were supposed to be bringing two folks back."

Big Jim didn't answer. Missy pushed the hound dog aside then climbed down the stairs. Jim stopped the wagon a few yards from the house. Missy's expression changed from curious to alarmed as she set her eyes on Patience.

"Oh, my Lord!" she said. "You sweet baby!"

Missy rushed to Patience then hugged her tight. Although she didn't know the woman, Patience felt safe for the first time since Papa died.

"Where's her daddy? Where's Maurice?"

"Haints got him," Jim said. "Patience said they took him on the ship and set it on fire in the process."

"Damn you, Jedediah!" Missy shouted, shaking her fist at the sky. She gently led Patience off the wagon.

"Your name is Patience, right?" she asked.

"Yes ma'am," Patience replied.

"I'm so sorry about what happened to your daddy," Missy said. "Things weren't supposed to transpire so soon. Let's go inside and get you something to eat."

Missy led Patience into her modest home. Inside a large iron stove burned with pots on the stove top. There was a table to the right of the stove and two rocking chairs before the fireplace. Missy continued to guide Patience through the large room into a smaller room opposite the entrance. Inside was a small bed with a dresser.

"You go on and lay down, baby," Missy said. "Supper's almost ready."

Missy eased Patience onto the bed then turned to leave. Patience gripped her hand.

"No," she said. "Don't leave me."

"Don't you want to get some rest?" Missy asked.

"Don't leave me," Patience repeated. "Don't leave me alone."

Missy's eyes widened as a sympathetic smile came to her face.

"You come on with me then," she said. "You can sit at the table while I finish cooking."

Patience trailed Missy into the kitchen then sat in one of the rocking chairs before the fireplace. Big Jim entered a few moments later, his thick arms cradling a stack of firewood. He placed the wood inside the fireplace then stacked the kindling. Patience watched then smiled as she imagined Poppa doing the same thing at their home, preparing the fire to cook a meal. Then the tears came again and she hid her face in her hands.

"You don't have to hide your tears, little lady," Big Jim said. "You been through a terrible time. Don't anybody expect you to feel otherwise."

"Come on over to the table, baby," Missy said.

"Which one of us you taking to?" Jim asked, a sly grin on his face.

"You wish," Missy said as she struggled to keep a cool demeanor. "Come over here, Patience. I got a hot bowl of gumbo for you."

"What about me?" Big Jim asked.

"You get to eat once you get that fire going, not before."

"You always working my nerves Missy," Big Jim complained. "Even when there's company."

"Especially when there's company," Missy replied.

A heavy knock drew their attention. Patience jumped from the rocker; her eyes filled with fear.

"It's alright," Missy said. "That's the twins. I was expecting them. Jimmy, get the door."

Patience watched Big Jim heave himself up from his chair and trudge to the door.

"Who is it?" he asked.

"Quit with your mess," a woman's voice answered. "Open the damn door."

"I swear that woman cusses like a sailor," Big Jim said.

Big Jim opened the door. A tall woman entered wearing a wide brim straw hat and a billowy cotton shirt. A black cotton skirt fell from her narrow waist to her boots. Her long neck was hidden by numerous beaded necklaces, some with bones, others with objects Patience didn't recognize. The woman carried a fiddle case in her left hand, a strange looking bow in her right. Her youthful countenance was marred by a wicked snarl until her eyes met Patience, then it was transformed by a warm smile.

"Hey there little lady!" she said. She was about to speak again when the door swung wide and the woman jumped aside.

"What's for supper?" a male voice rumbled.

A man entered, just as tall as the woman but stout like a dock worker. Sweat beaded on his bald head, as his yellow eyes darted back and forth before centering on the pots simmering on the stove. He licked his lips as he rubbed his large hands together. He wore a white shirt like the woman, the sleeves rolled up to his massive biceps. Ivory machete handles peeked over each shoulder. A pair of worn dungarees struggled to hold his thick legs, each muscle visible as he strode across the room toward Missy. His eyes fell on Patience and he stopped then squatted before her, his hands resting on his thighs. Patience held her breath for a moment until a smile as warm as the woman's came to his face.

"What's your name?" he asked.

"Patience," she said.

The man extended his hand; Patience placed her hand in his and it disappeared inside his grip. She expected his handshake to be harsh; instead it was as gentle as his smile.

"Pleased to meet you, Patience. I'm Courtney Brimstone."

The woman joined them.

"I'm Corliss Brimstone."

Patience swallowed before replying. "Pleased to meet you both."

Courtney nodded then stood.

"Now that introductions are out of the way, where's the food?"

"You ain't got no good words for me?" Missy said.

Corliss and Cornelius rushed over to Missy and the three shared a group hug. Courtney pulled away from the hug then motioned his head toward Patience.

"Ain't we missing somebody?" he asked.

"We'll talk about that later," Missy said.

"No need to talk," Corliss said. "Haints done already told me."

Patience looked at Corliss and saw the knowledge in her eyes. She began to cry again. Corliss came to her then wrapped her in her long arms. The embrace felt familiar, like a hug she would expect from the big sister she never had.

"Hard times about to come," she whispered. "But you're going to be alright. I promise."

"They killed my papa," Patience said.

"I know baby, I know," Corliss replied. "I felt it. But let me tell you something. Your papa may be dead, but he ain't gone."

Corliss words stopped Patience's crying.

"What do you mean, Miss Corliss?" she asked.

Corliss brushed a stray hair from Patience's face.

"You'll see. But right now, let's get some food in that empty belly of yours."

Patience was about to protest when a hunger pang caused her stomach to clinch. She looked at Corliss in wonder and the woman smiled.

"Come on now. Let's eat."

"Yes, Miss Corliss," Patience replied.

"Just Corliss," the woman said. "You and I are going to be sisters."

Courtney frowned. "Last thing we need is more family."

"Hush up, Peanut," Corliss said. "Sit your hungry ass at the table and be quiet."

Patience covered her mouth to muffle her laughter. Corliss winked at her.

"That's how you have to handle him," she said. "You'll learn."

Patience took Corliss's hand then followed her to the table. Missy filled the bowls with steaming gumbo which Patience and the others ate with relish. She didn't realize how hungry she was until the spicy and savory mix met her lips. By the time she finished cleaning her bowl with cornbread Missy had filled her plate with collard greens, red rice and fried fish. The table fell silent as everyone indulged in the delicious meal. For the time being Patience didn't think of the tragic events that had just occurred; she enjoyed the moment with her new friends.

Courtney was the first to finish. He pushed away from the table, leaned his chair onto the back legs then rubbed his stomach.

"Lordy, Lordy that was some good food!" he said. "Good thing I can't eat this way every day or I'd be big as Jimmy."

"You about big as me right now eating them damn roots," Big Jim shot back. Missy slapped him across the head and he winced.

"No swearing at the dinner table," she said.

"He's big because he eats roots like a cow," Corliss said.

"Well I'm glad y'all enjoyed the meal," Missy said. "But it's time we talked about serious matters."

Patience stiffened. Everyone at the table looked at her. She knew what was coming next.

"Tell us what happened, baby," Missy said. "Tell us everything."

Patience closed her eyes then described the scene to them. By the time she was done tears ran down her cheeks. Corliss moved her chair beside her then wrapped her arms around her. Just like before her touch was extremely soothing.

"'I'm so sorry you had to be there," she said. "Your daddy is a brave man."

"Why did they kill him?" she blurted between sobs. "Why? He never hurt anyone!"

Missy shifted closer to Patience.

"Sweety, your daddy is a soldier in a war that started a long, long time ago, way before you or any of us was born. He knew what was coming and was ready to fight and die for it."

Patience looked into Missy's eyes. She saw the seriousness of the woman and it gave her strength.

"Papa gave me his bois," she said. "He told me to make sure Miss Tubman got it."

"Can you show it to me?" Missy asked.

Patience left the table and went to the room where she'd left her things. She picked up the box containing the bois then brought it into the kitchen. She gave it to Missy. When Missy took it in her hands she swayed. Big Jim jumped from his seat but Missy waved him away.

"I'm alright," she said. Missy handed the box back to Patience.

"Can you open this for me?"

Patience hesitated. "Papa never allowed me to touch it."

"It's yours now," Missy said. "Open it."

Patience unlatched the lid then opened the box. The bois lay cradled in an indigo velvet cushion, an ebony stick covered with elaborate carvings. Patience touched the stick and a tingling passed from her hands and throughout her body. She shuddered.

Courtney moved closer; disappointment clear on his face.

"That's all? A pretty stick?"

"It's more than that," Missy said. "It's a talisman, just like your root bag and Corliss's fiddle. But it's older, much older. And it's got the ashé of powerful ancestors inside."

"Ashé?" Corliss asked.

Missy nodded. "Ashé is the essence giving to every living thing by Olodumare, the supreme god of our ancestors. This bois was made long ago, when our people knew who they were and still spoke the language of our home."

"Shoot, that ain't nothing," Courtney said. "I speak the language of my home. Beaufort, South Carolina."

"Shut up fool and listen," Corliss said.

Missy ran her hands over the bois, her eyes shut tight.

"Yes, yes," she said, her voice almost a whisper. "I see them. I see them all."

"Who do you see?" Patience asked.

"I see your family," Missy said. "I see your lineage back to the Motherland and beyond. They are all here."

"Are my mama and papa here?" she asked.

"You will find out soon enough," Missy answered.

Missy handed the bois back to Patience. Patience placed it back into the case and closed it.

"I think I'll go to bed now," Patience said. Missy opened her mouth but Corliss shook her head.

"You get some rest, Patience," Corliss said.

Patience wrapped her arms around the box then hurried into the room. She lay in the bed then cried silently while the others talked in the next room. Missy had given her hope; she thought the woman would tell her something about her parents. *You will find out soon enough*, she said. How soon? Patience wondered. How soon?

THREE

"Patience."

Patience jumped upright in the bed, bumping against someone. She turned to see Corliss beside her, her breathing heavy. She was about to touch the woman to see what she wanted when she heard the voice again.

"Patience."

This time she recognized it.

"Papa! Papa, where are you?"

"There's not much time, cheri," he said. *"They are coming. You must warn the others."*

"Who is coming, Papa? Who?"

"The ones that killed me," Papa said. *"They are coming for you."*

Patience sat in a daze, trying to comprehend what was happening to her.

"Patience, you must wake up your friends," Papa said.

"Papa, how are you…"

"PATIENCE! WAKE UP YOUR FRIENDS NOW!"

Patience grabbed Corliss's shoulders then shook her as hard as she could. Corliss eyes popped open.

"Chile, what are you doing?" she said

"Papa told me to wake you," Patience said. "He said they are coming."

"They?" Corliss's eyes went wide. She jumped from the bed.

"Everybody wake up!" she shouted. "Haints are coming!"

The little house exploded in activity. Courtney came to his feet as if he'd never been asleep, his machetes drawn. Big Jim blocked the door holding an axe, his thick hands twisting on the handle. Missy stood in the center of the house, her eyes closed and her arms extended. She seemed to be chanting. Patience watched in amazement as her fingertips began to glow, the light becoming so intense that they illuminated the room like daylight. Corliss joined Courtney, fiddle in one hand, bow in the other. Everyone looked at Missy. When the woman finally lifted her head, her eyes glowed like her fingertips.

"Go," she said, her luminous eyes focused on the twins. "Take Patience. Keep her safe."

"I ain't running from no haints!" Courtney shouted.

"This ain't your fight," Missy said. "Me and Jimmy will handle this. Now go!"

Corliss looked at Patience and shared one of her calming smiles.

"Get your things, chile," she said. "And take out that stick of yours. You might need to use it."

Patience stuffed her clothes in her bag then secured it on her back. She opened the box and took out Papa's bois. The stick felt warm in her hand, pulsing with the rhythm of her heart.

"Are you ready, cheri," her father said.

"I'm afraid," she replied.

"Don't be," Papa said. *"We are with you."*

"Come on, girl!" Courtney shouted. "We go to go."

Patience ran from the room to Corliss's side. The group was gathered in the center of the room, everyone's eyes on Missy. The kind woman had taken on a serene look, as if she was far away. It was the same look Papa had when he stood in the flames. Patience's hands trembled.

"Take the north highway to the ford," Missy said. "Old Man Jones will get you to the mainland. Once you get there, head west along Terminus Highway. About five miles down the road you'll come across train tracks. A train will come around noon. It will be traveling slowly with a load of pulpwood. You should be able to jump on and ride it to Dublin. You'll have to change trains there to take you west."

Corliss raised her head.

"They're getting close," she said.

"We need more time," Missy replied. "You better play something."

Corliss let go of Patience's hand.

"You better cover your ears," she said. "The first time is usually pretty rough."

Corliss tucked the fiddle under her chin then raised the bow. Patience cupped her hands over her ears as she was told. The others closed their eyes then stood rigid. Corliss dragged the bow over the strings. The sound created was not music. A sharp pain struck Patience's stomach and her hands clutched at the ache as she fell to her knees. It was the worst she'd ever felt, like she was being stabbed by fire. Her scream was drowned out by louder cries from outside the house, sounds that could not have come from the throats of humans. The agony in her gut subsided as quickly as it had come, but the cries outside continued as Corliss played. They eventually faded into the distance and Corliss stopped playing.

Courtney came to Patience then helped her to her feet.

"How you feeling?" he asked.

"Terrible," Patience replied.

"She did better than I expected," Missy said. "She's strong."

Corliss hugged her then kissed her cheek, taking the pain away.

"I'm sorry, chile," she said. "It takes Siren a minute to get to know you. You'll be alright the next time."

Patience struggled to her feet.

"Siren?"

Corliss raised the fiddle. "That's what I call her."

"You need to leave now," Missy said. "They'll be back."

Patience gazed into Missy's eyes.

"You aren't coming."

"No sugar," Missy said. "This is your journey. Mine is done."

The way she said those words told Patience she would never see Missy and Big Jim again.

Courtney and Corliss hugged Missy and Big Jim. Patience hugged them as well, the sorrow she felt as deep as for people she had known all her life.

"Missy," she said. "Why is this happening?"

Missy smiled, her eyes still glowing.

"Because it always has chile," she said.

"We're wasting time," Courtney said. "Come on, gal."

Patience kissed Missy's cheek then marched to the twins.

"I'm ready," she said.

"No, you ain't," Courtney replied. "But it don't make no difference now. Stay between me and Corliss, you hear?"

"Yes," Patience answered.

Courtney took his root bag from his pocket. He opened it then sprinkled the contents about the house, and then he ran to the door and snatched it open. He darted outside, Patience and Corliss following. They ran down the path leading from the house then onto the main road. A sound like hurricane winds rose behind them; Patience looked back to see a gray mass twisting around Missy's house, a mass of distorted human like shapes. A portion of the mass broke away and surged in their direction.

"Run Patience!" Corliss yelled.

Patience ran as fast as she could but still could not catch up to Courtney. She felt Corliss hand press against her back, pushing her to move faster. She peeked over her shoulder again; the gray mass was closing on them.

"This ain't going to work," Corliss shouted. "She ain't fast enough!"

"I'm glad you said that," Courtney shouted back. Courtney ran a bit further into an open stretch on the road then stopped. He reached into his pocket, extracting another root bag. Corliss eyes went wide when she saw the bag.

"You sure?" she said.

"Yep," Courtney replied.

Corliss looked at Patience.

"Get down on the ground," she said. "Stay there till I tell you to get up."

"Yes ma'am!" Patience replied. She sat on the ground, clutching her Papa's bois. The gray swarm finally reached them, a foul howling invading Patience's ears as the mass descended toward them. Courtney looked upward, a mischievous smile on his face. Corliss looked up as well, her fiddle braced against her chin, her bow poised over the strings. Courtney threw the root bag into the cloud. It spun, caught in the mass then opened, changing the cloud from gray to black.

"Now!" he shouted.

Corliss dragged her bow over the strings, producing a high-pitched note. Patience was blinded by intense light then there was an explosion that pushed her into the ground. She lay still for what seemed like minutes, stunned by the force.

"Get up, cheri," she heard her father say. *"You must help them."*

Patience struggled to her feet as her eyes and ears cleared. What she saw struck her with terror. The ground around her was littered with misshapen creatures, some writhing, others still. Those still alive and undamaged attacked Courtney and Corliss. The twins stood back-to-back, wielding their machetes against the relentless attack. Patience walked toward them, her bois held high as her father taught her. Suddenly the bois pulled her toward the fray, almost dragging her to one of the beasts. Her hand slid to the base of the bois and she swung down, splitting the creature's skull. Gray ichor splashed her clothes and face, stinging her bare skin. Patience attempted to run away but the bois would not let her. It pulled her to the next creature then guided her hands to strike it on the back of the thighs. The creature fell backwards; Patience took off its head with a blow to its neck. The bois continued to take her from ghoul to ghoul until none remained alive. Patience panted, more from fear than fatigue. When she looked at Courtney and Corliss, they were covered in ghoul blood, looking at her with smiles.

"Damn, girl," Courtney said. "You did good!"

Patience looked at them, her hands trembling.

"I didn't do this," she stammered. "Papa did."

Courtney looked and Corliss.

"What the hell is she talking about? Her daddy is . . ."

A loud explosion cut him off, the force knocking the three of them to the ground. The bois flew from Patience's hands as she tumbled over the ground, coming to a stop against Corliss. She immediately jumped to her feet to find it but another sight took her attention. A fire blazed where Missy's house had once stood, the ground littered with the charred bodies of ghouls. She felt a soothing touch on her shoulder and knew it was Corliss.

"Come on, baby," she said. "We have to get moving."

Patience looked into Corliss's eyes. Corliss shared a melancholy smile.

"You know what happened," she said.

Corliss handed her the bois.

"Here's your stick. We need to be getting on now. This ain't the last of the haints."

FOUR

Corliss, Patience and Courtney hurried away from the devastation, running until they reached the ford. They were too late; Old Man Jones had shut down the ferry for the day, the flat-bottomed craft chained to a nearby persimmon tree. Not that it mattered to Patience; she had no idea who the man was. She hoped Corliss and Courtney would recognize him.

"We'll camp here tonight," Courtney said. "No fires."

They found a stand of pine trees next to the Spanish moss draped canopy of an old live oak. Corliss and Courtney began piling leaves and pine needles and Patience followed their example. Once done the twins laid on their natural beds. Patience did the same. As soon as she settled Courtney came to her, root bag in hand. He took out a strip of bark then handed it to her.

"What is it?" Patience asked.

"Willow bark," Courtney replied. "Eases the pain. I added a little something to help you sleep."

Patience looked at Corliss.

"Why you looking at her?" Courtney asked. "She ain't got nothing to do with this."

Corliss laughed. "After seeing what you did to them haints, I'd look at me, too. Poor thing probably thinks you're going to blow her up."

"Now why the hell would I do that?"

"Watch your mouth!" Corliss said. "We have a child with us now. Can't be talking any kind of way."

"It's okay," Patience said. "I spent a lot of time on the docks with Papa. Men say the most horrible things."

Corliss laughed. "Yes, they do."

"So now y'all gonna gang up on me? Give me my willow bark back."

Patience giggled as she stuffed the bark in her mouth and chewed. Courtney grinned.

"There you go. You'll be feeling right better soon."

Patience chewed the bitter bark and slowly felt her pain subside. She realized that the twins' banter was for her sake. They were trying to minimize the horrible situation they'd just experienced. It worked to a certain extent. She wasn't a child. She knew Missy and Big Jim died in the explosion and that they knew they would have to sacrifice themselves so she and the twins could escape. She thought of Papa, how he stood in the fire and didn't attempt to leave, telling her he loved her as he was consumed. Then she looked at the box where Papa's bois rested. Was it really so important to be worth so many lives?

She felt her eyes getting heavy, so she laid down on her leaves and pine needles. Sleep came quickly; she awoke to her old room, lying in her bed all tucked in. Sitting at the foot of her bed was Papa.

"Papa!" she shouted. "We're home!"

"I wish that was true, Cheri," Papa said, his voice heavy with sadness.

"So, this is not real," she said.

"No."

"It's a dream."

Papa smiled. *"No."*

Patience was dumbfounded. "Then what is it?"

"Something in between."

"Why can't you come back, Papa," Patience asked.

"I have."

"I mean all the way back."

Papa's smile faded. *"It doesn't work that way, Cheri. Once we move on, we can't come back. There are . . . changes that can't be reversed."*

"I miss you so much," she said.

"I miss you, too."

Patience sat up in the bed.

"Have you seen mama?" she asked.

The question brought a smile to Papa's face which made Patience smile despite her sadness.

"Not yet," he answered. *"Your mama is in a different place, a place that once I travel*

there, I won't be able to return. For now, I'm here with you."

Patience tilted her head. "Why?"

"There were many things I meant to teach you," he said. *"You must know about the bois and its abilities. You are part of a legacy that extends to the Motherland. My bois is a powerful talisman and will be very useful in the upcoming struggle."*

"I don't want to fight, Papa," she said. "All I want to do is give Miss Tubman the bois then go home."

"The bois is useless unless it's in your hands," Papa said. *"You are the link between the bois and our ancestors. It's through you that the bois manifests its power."*

"You were supposed to use it, not me!" Patience shouted. "It's not fair!"

"You are right, Cheri. It was I who was supposed to wield the bois. And it's not fair that you must stand in my stead. But this is a very serious situation, and very few people can prevent it. You are one of those people."

"But you said yourself that I'm not ready."

"You're not, but you will be. Let the bois guide you. Let it have its way. You will learn through its movement, and you will learn from Courtney and Corliss. They are much older than they seem. When you have questions, I will be here, just as I am now."

"Okay papa," Patience answered. "I will do as you say."

"Good. Now go back to sleep. Tomorrow will be a long day."

The images faded around her, leaving the wooded darkness in its place. Patience didn't think she could sleep after her experience, but she fell asleep as soon as her head touched the leaves. She awoke to the most beautiful music she'd ever heard. Corliss sat nearby, playing her fiddle. Until that point Patience didn't think the instrument was capable of such sounds. She watched Corliss play; her eyes closed as she swayed with the rhythm of the tune. Patience began to sway with her and before she knew it, she was on her feet and dancing, humming the tune.

"Well now, we have a dancer with us!"

Courtney's voice broke her reverie. She stumbled to a halt.

"No, keep on dancing," he said.

Patience looked away, embarrassed.

"Maybe this will help," he said.

Courtney took out a drum with strings connecting the top and bottom drumhead. He tucked the drum under his arm then took out a stick with a curved head. He began to beat the drum in time with Corliss's playing, squeezing his arm against the string and changing the pitch of the drum. Courtney was right; the drumming and fiddling moved her to dance again. She danced until they stopped, her forehead glistening with sweat.

"You just full of surprises," Courtney said.

"I ain't surprised," Corliss replied. "I could feel she was a dancer."

Corliss's words sparked the question she'd been meaning to ask her new-found sister.

"How do you know?" she said.

Corliss opened her fiddle case. "How do I know what?"

Patience walked closer. "How do you know how I feel? You always say the right thing."

Corliss smiled. "It's my calling. I feel what you feel."

"But how do you do it?" Patience asked.

"I don't know," Corliss replied. "It's my nyama; my gift. At first, I was afraid of it. But I learned how to control it. Now I use it help girls that are in a strange land missing their father."

Corliss's words should have made Patience sad, but they didn't. She knew her father was still with her, and she felt Corliss's words weren't meant to hurt.

"Is fiddle playing your calling, too?"

"No. I learned that from my grandmama. That woman could play the angels down from Heaven. She taught me how to make my own fiddle and how to play. When she died, I played a song so sad it rained for a week."

"Sho'nuff did," Courtney said. "That girl made the angels cry."

"Didn't mean to," Corliss said.

"But it makes terrible sounds too," Patience added.

Corliss's smile faded.

"Yes, it does, Patience. Yes, it does."

"Did your daddy teach you how to fight with that stick?" Courtney asked.

"Bois," Patience said.

"What?"

"It's called a bois," Patience said. "And yes, my papa taught me. We would practice on the docks after his work was done. We would sing a song while we played."

"Can you sing it now?" Corliss asked.

Patience looked into Corliss's eyes and found the strength. She opened her box and took out Papa's bois. She held the stick with both hands over her head then sang.

Mooma, Mooma
Your son in de grave already,
Your son in de grave already,
Take a towel and ban you belly,
Mooma, Mooma,
Today is your son's burial,
Today is your son's burial,
Tomorrow is a grand funeral...

Her voice was weak and shaky as she remembered Papa. Then a strange thing occurred. The air before her wavered, a misty shape rising before her. The mist seemed to move with the rhythm of her words. Her voice became stronger as the mist took shape. Suddenly Patience gazed on the image of her father. She began to scream but Papa raised his finger to his mouth. Patience sang strong and loud as Papa kept time with her, his empty hands matching her movements with the bois.

Mooma, Mooma
Your son in de grave already,
Your son in de grave already,
Take a towel and ban you belly,
Mooma, Mooma,
Today is your son's burial,
Today is your son's burial,
Tomorrow is a grand funeral…

Courtney and Corliss entered her view, dancing on either side of Papa as if they knew he was there. Courtney lumbered about, keeping time in a stiff sort of way, while Corliss danced with a grace that didn't surprise Patience one bit. Courtney took up the rhythm on his drum and Corliss pluck her strings in time.

Mooma, Mooma,
Your son in de grave already,
Your son in de grave already,
Take a towel and ban your belly.
Mooma, Mooma,
Today is the grand funeral,
Today is the grand funeral,
Next time it's the grand burial!

Patience sang the song over again. Courtney and Corliss were fast learners; they sang and played with her. As they reached the end of the song Papa looked into her eyes.

"I told you I would be with you as long as you need me," he said.

Patience smiled as he faded away.

"Now that was fun," Courtney said.

"Yes, it was," Corliss replied. "We'll have to add this tune to our collection."

Courtney looked up into the sky then frowned.

"We best be getting on," he said. "According to Missy that train will be coming along soon. If we miss it today, we'll have to wait until tomorrow."

"Let's go then," Corliss answered.

The three of them gathered their things then headed toward the train tracks.

* * *

The beasts approached the smoldering pit warily, there wet noses flaring as they sniffed for spectral spoor. Their master released them miles ago, allowing them to hunt without his stern restrictions. There were bodies in their wake, those unfortunate to be in their path as they hunted. This was their true target, but those who they sought were gone.

Their master emerged from the woods; his massive body barely contained by the bloody overalls he wore. He too had hunted, leaving death and terror that would be remembered for decades afterwards. The beasts howled when they saw him, a horrifying acknowledgement of his presence. He walked to the edge of the pit then squatted. His hands hovered over the ground for a moment then he snatched them away as if burned.

"Are they dead?" the voice asked.

The hound master's throat tightened, a hint of fear in his eyes. He too had a master.

"The witch and her henchman are," he answered. "There is no sign of the others."

"Find them. Kill them. They must not reach the Artifact."

The hound master inserted his fingers into his mouth and whistled. The hounds gathered around him, whimpering and wagging for his attention like pups. He closed his eyes and transferred the image of those they hunted into the hounds' simple minds. Then he whistled again, a short sharp note that carried over the charred field. The hounds answered then raced ahead into the darkness.

FIVE

The battered pulpwood steam train squealed to a halt at the lumber camp, prepared to take on another load of timber destined for the paper mills of central Georgia. It would require the remainder of the day to load the stripped pine trunks, so the train crews would spend the night in the camp before setting off in the morning with full loads. In addition to wood, a few cars were reserved for livestock and grain. It was the grain cars Courtney, Corliss and Patience were interested in.

Patience stifled a burp as they observed the camp. The rabbits Courtney killed and cooked made a great meal in combination with the wild greens she and Corliss gathered. What they didn't eat they did their best to smoke to carry as provisions. Once the train got moving it would be unpredictable when and where it would stop, so they had to make sure they had their own supplies.

"Best get some rest now," Courtney said. "If you ain't used to sleeping on a train you won't get much rest. Once we reach Atlanta, we'll stay in the city for a few days to raise some money."

"How are we going to do that?" Patience asked.

"With our playing and your singing and dancing we should do pretty good," Corliss said.

Patience's stomach fluttered. "I'm not sure I can sing and dance in front of a crowd."

"Sure, you can!" Corliss said. "Just close your eyes and feel the music like you did with us. Of course, you don't have to do it unless you want to."

"Yes, she does," Courtney said. "Everybody has to pull their own weight. This ain't no charity."

"You forgetting who she is," Corliss said.

"I know exactly who she is. Pardon me saying but she ain't her daddy. He was who we were expecting."

Patience stood.

"I wish he was here too," she said. "But he's not. I'll pull my weight. Don't worry about me. Just get us on that train."

Corliss laughed. "That's how you handle him, Patience!"

Courtney frowned. "Sit down before somebody sees you. And get some rest."

Patience settled as well as she could on the hard ground. She didn't think she could sleep but she did, even without Courtney's root medicine. She awoke a few times to see either Courtney or Corliss watching over her as they carried out some mundane task. As darkness settled over them the three of them slept.

She was awakened by Corliss's voice.

"Come on, Patience!" she said. "It's time!"

The trio rose from their hiding place then sprinted down the hill toward the slowly moving train. Courtney was the first to reach the empty cattle car. He climbed onto the car then opened the sliding door. Corliss grabbed Patience under her arms then lifted her high; Courtney grabbed her outstretched hands then pulled her inside. He grabbed Corliss's hands moments later then lifted her into the car as well.

The smell was terrible. Patience covered her mouth and nose with her hands, but the odor seeped through her fingers. The stench was so terrible she could taste it. She thought she would throw up at any moment.

Courtney handed her a cloth with strings hanging from either end.

"Tie this around your mouth and nose," he said. "It'll kill the smell."

Patience snatched the cloth from his hand and tied it around her face as fast as she could. It made a great difference, minimizing the odor although not eliminating it. Corliss and Courtney did the same.

"It smells terrible in here," Patience complained.

"It ain't that bad," Corliss said. "You're just a city girl. You ain't used to smells like this."

"Yep," Courtney agreed as he settled against the car wall. "If you grew up on a farm you would be."

"How can you get used to this?"

"By the time we get off this train you will be. Settle in; it's going to be a long ride."

Patience didn't share with the twins that this was her first train ride; she was too distracted by their odiferous situation to mention it. There was no way out of except for them to reach their destination, which couldn't happen soon enough. Missy chose this train because it had the fewest stops between the Low Country and Atlanta. Patience found it hard to eat but forced herself so she wouldn't get weak or hungry. Eventually she became used the constant rhythm of the train. After a few hours the sound lulled her to sleep.

Patience felt the train come to a stop then opened her eyes. Courtney and Corliss were gathering their things.

"This is where we get off," Corliss said. "There's a town nearby with a passenger train station. That train will take us to Atlanta. They have a Negro car, but it'll be a few days before it arrives. We'll have to make do until then."

"Where are we going to stay?" Patience asked.

"Wherever we can," Courtney asked. "We'll put on a little performance and see what that gets us."

"I'll have to sing and dance?"

Corliss smiled. "Yes ma'am!"

Patience cringed.

They hopped off the train then Patience trudged behind the twins into town. It wasn't much of a place; three wooden buildings cloistered together near the train tracks. As they neared the dwellings, the door of one of center buildings opened and a white man in a black suit and wearing a wide brim hat stepped out. The man cradled a shotgun in his arms and a star-shaped badge glinted on his chest.

"Damn," Courtney said. "Ain't even settled good, and trouble comes walking our way."

"Stay calm," Corliss said. "He's just going to shoo us along. We'll ask him where the Negroes live and be on our way."

The sheriff stopped a few feet away from them.

"I seen y'all jump off that train," he said. "We don't need no train jumpers around here so y'all keep on moving."

"We were just looking for a place for folks like us to stay," Corliss said.

"Ain't one," the white man said. "We got some good Negroes around here that don't need to be associating the likes of you."

"But you don't even know us!" Patience said.

The man looked around Corliss to Patience, who drew back from his stare. Never had someone looked at her with such hate in their eyes.

"She didn't mean nothing," Corliss said. "She ain't from around here. We'll be moving on as soon as the next train comes through."

"Well get on then," the man said.

Courtney looked at Corliss and she nodded.

"Excuse me sir," he said. "It there somewhere we can wash ourselves?"

The sheriff's face hardened. He marched up to Courtney until their noses almost touched.

"Buck, did you hear me? I said I want you three to . . ."

Courtney's hand move so fast Patience barely saw it. The man's head was swallowed by a white cloud of powder. He gagged and coughed for what seemed like forever while Courtney and Corliss looked about nervously. The man finally stopped coughing. His hateful expression faded away, replaced by a blank stare.

"What's your name?" Courtney asked.

"Percy Lakebottom," the man answered in a curious monotone.

"Percy, where do the Negroes live in this shit hole?" Courtney asked.

"Courtney!" Corliss said. She cut her eyes at Patience.

Courtney shrugged then turned his attention back to Percy.

"Well? Answer my question!"

The man's left arm lifted stiffly then he pointed to the railroad tracks."

"That way," he said. "In Pineyville."

"Much obliged," Courtney said. "Now I want you to walk back to your office and take a long nap. Don't wake up until hear the passenger train departure whistle, you hear?"

The man nodded his head.

"Git on now!"

Sheriff Lakebottom staggered to his office. Courtney, Patience and Corliss fast walked in the direction the sheriff pointed out.

"You shouldn't have done that," Corliss said. "When he comes out of it, he's going to be madder than a hornet."

"He deserved it, red-neck bastard," Courtney replied. "Sorry, Patience."

Courtney grinned. "Besides, by the time he comes to we'll be long gone."

"What did he do?" Patience asked Corliss.

"Why you keep asking her my questions?" Courtney said. "I'm standing right here."

Patience smiled. "What did you do?"

"Let Corliss tell you. You asked her first."

Corliss laughed. "You're such a baby. He used his make-do power on him."

"Make-do powder?" Patience was puzzled.

"Yeah. It makes folks do what you want them to. Only problem is that once they come out of it, they remember everything they did and who made them do it."

"I ain't perfected it yet," Courtney said. "We'll be long gone before ol' Percy finds his mind."

"I hope so," Corliss said. "Come on, let's get washed up then see if anyone will let us sit a spell and give us a good meal."

They traveled to the creek. It was a dingy trickle of water, but enough for them to wash their faces and hands and get rid of the cattle smell clinging to their clothes and body. Afterwards, they sauntered to Pineyville. The town, if it could be called such, was in worse shape than the white section of town. The dilapidated train station was abandoned, and the nearby building was charred from a previous fire. Patience looked off in the distance. She saw many farmhouses and fields, the fields occupied by working hands.

"I don't think this is going to work," she said. "Everyone is working too far away."

"You'll be surprised how far the sound of a well-played drum and fiddle will carry," Courtney said. "You just be ready to add that pretty voice of yours when I tell you to."

Corliss took out her fiddle, braced it against her chest then struck the string with her bow, emitting a long, sweet note that seemed to reach all the way to Glory. Patience observed the farmers stop whatever they were doing to look in their direction. Courtney belted out a fast rhythm and the two played a tune that set Patience's feet to moving. She was dancing before she realized it, summoned by the music being laid down by the twins. This had to be hoodoo, she thought as she twirled, dipped and shook.

"Watch that waist twisting!" Courtney shouted. "Folks round here might take that the wrong way."

"I will!" Patience shouted back.

She was so immersed in the music that she never noticed the crowd forming a circle around them.

"Time to sing, songbird," Corliss said.

Patience didn't need any further prompting. Papa's song sprang from her throat full and strong with an energy she'd never felt. The crowd clapped, a few pairing off to dance. She watched Corliss join them, dancing and playing and laughing with the crowd. Patience laughed as she turned toward Courtney; he smiled at her then motioned for her to look behind her. A good distance away a crowd of white people gathered, bobbing their heads and doing their best to imitate the dancing of the Negroes.

"Take my hat," he said to Patience. She jumped and grabbed his hat as he bent forward in time to the music.

"Now dance yourself over to them white folks," Courtney said. "Make sure you say thank you sir or ma'am for every penny."

"Yes sir!" Patience sang. She skipped over to the white people then danced. They dropped their coins into the hat, grinning as she pranced and curtseyed among them. Then she skipped away to the Negroes, who parted with their coins just as easily. The hat heavy with coins, Courtney winked at Corliss, and they closed the song with a rousing crescendo. The onlookers clapped long and loud; after a few minutes both white people and Negroes dispersed, their momentary unity over.

One man lingered; an old Negro man covered in dirty overalls. He shared a welcoming smile with them as he approached.

"Been a long time since I heard music that good," he said. He extended his hand to Corliss.

"Name's Samuel Birdsong," he said. "Folks 'round here call me Sammy Bird."

Corliss shook his hand. "I'm Corliss Brimstone. That's my brother Courtney and this right here–she pointed at Patience–is our little sister Patience."

Sammy Bird shook Courtney's hand then tipped his hat to Patience.

"What brings y'all to Pineyville?"

"Just passing through," Corliss said.

"Where y'all headed?"

"Atlanta. Since the next train was going to take a while, we decided to try to make little extra money. You never know what the road has in store for you."

"I'll have to take your word for it," Sammy Bird replied. "I ain't never been much of a traveling sort. I ain't got any money to spare, but I can offer y'all some good food and some fresh clothes while you wait on the train."

Courtney rubbed his chin. "We appreciate your offer Sammy Bird, but I don't think we're going to have the time. The train will be coming soon."

Sammy waved his hand. "That train is always late. Come on with me. After all that dancing and playing and singing y'all bound to be hungry."

"I could eat a little something," Corliss said.

"Me, too!" Patience added.

"I guess I'm overruled," Courtney said. "Lead the way, sir."

The trio followed Sammy down the dirt road to the first farm on the right. The fields were fallow, the red clay soil freshly plowed. Sammy's house was bigger than most, shaded by two live oaks that canopies tangled overhead like lover's hands. They followed Sammy up the porch stairs, through the screen door and into the modest home.

"Mama Bird, they're here!" shouted out.

"I'll be right in," a female voice called back. "Killing a few chickens for them."

"You don't have to do that," Corliss said.

Mama Bird entered the house through the back door. She was a petite woman, no taller that Patience, with a charcoal complexion and a wide smile. She wore a simple linen dress and a flowered head wrap, the dress stained by the blood from the chickens she held in her left hand. The butcher knife in her right hand dripped blood. But what Patience noticed was her eyes. Her dark pupils were obscured by a white film. She was blind.

Sammy sauntered over to Mama Bird then took the chickens from her hand.

"I'll finish them up," he said.

"Thank you, Sammy," she said. "I'm so glad y'all are here. Come on sit down."

Mama Bird walked to the kitchen table, pulled out a seat and sat. Corliss and Courtney did the same. Patience didn't move.

"Come on over here girl," Mama Bird said. "I ain't gonna bite you."

"Yes . . . yes ma'am." Patience came to the table and sat.

"Don't stare," Corliss said. "It ain't polite."

"That's alright," Mama Bird said. "Most people do when they first meet me. I'm used to it."

"How do you know they're staring?" Patience asked.

Mama Bird laughed then reached out and patted Patience's hand.

"I can see better than anybody," she said. "I see what's inside."

"This would go a lot faster if I had some help," Sammy called out.

"I'll do the honors," Courtney said. "Got no problem working for a meal."

"Now that the men folk are doing the work, we women can do some serious talking," Mama Bird said. "I seen y'all coming for a few days now. I was wondering if y'all were going to pass us by. Thank Providence you didn't."

A knowing smile came to Corliss's face. "You're a special woman, Mama Bird."

"Not as special as you three." She patted Patience's hand. "Especially you. That's a powerful stick you're carrying."

"How did you know?" Patience asked.

"I've been blind from birth," Mama Bird said. "I can't see with my eyes, but I can see with my soul. This kind of sight carries a lot farther and reveals a lot more."

"We're traveling to a place where folks like us can help people be free," Corliss said. "You and Sammy should come with us."

Mama Bird laughed. "Ain't my time yet. Folks like you got to pave the way. I do have something to give you, though."

Mama Bird left the table, disappearing into the small bedroom. She returned with a small white box.

"My grandma gave this to me," Mama Bird said. "She said it came from Africa, but how her mama brought it over on them slave ships without it being took is beyond me. But I can feel the spirits in it, so I know it's right. When you get to where you going, you give this to Miss Tubman. Tell her Mama Bird sent it."

"I surely will," Corliss said. She took the box then placed it in her fiddle case. Mama Bird then turned to Patience. Her soft demeanor stiffened.

"What you have is powerful girl," she said. "Keep it close and listen to it. You have a lot to learn."

"Yes ma'am," Patience said.

"I got these chickens ready to go," Sammy said. His presence shifted Mama Bird's mood; she smiled and patted Patience's hand.

"I reckon it's my turn," she said.

"I'll help," Corliss said.

"Me, too," Patience said.

"Y'all come on then!"

The three of them made the work easy. Patience felt warm inside; she remembered when she and Papa would cook together. The warmness soon gave way to sadness and tears formed in her eyes. She felt Corliss's arm slide over her shoulders.

"Why don't you go sit down," Corliss said. "Me and Mama Bird can handle this."

Patience wiped her eyes. "No. I want to help. I have to help."

"Okay baby. Why don't you grease those pans for the biscuits?"

Patience did as she was told, the pain easing as she concentrated on her task. She was almost done when Mama Bird appeared beside her.

"I can smell that dress you're wearing, and it don't smell good," she said.

"It's all I have," Patience replied. "I've been meaning to wash it but haven't had the time."

"I tell you what. How about you wash your hands and come with me. I got something to show you."

Patience cleaned the lard off her hands then followed Mama Bird to a small room next to the bedroom. Inside was a wash tub, an ironing board, and a small table. Piled against the walls were clothes; pants, shirts, dresses and skirts.

"I do the washing for white folks and Negroes around here," Mama Bird said. "Sometimes they leave their old clothes or those they don't like. I'm sure there's something in here that fits you. Whatever you find, it's yours."

"Thank you, Mama Bird!"

Patience decided to pick out boy's clothes instead of the usual dress or skirt. She figured it was easier to travel in pants than in a skirt. When she came back into the kitchen she was met with a host of reactions. Corliss smiled; Mister Sammy frowned; Courtney laughed out loud.

"Well look-a-here," Courtney said. "Our Patience has become Paul."

"No I haven't!" Patience said. "I just think pants will be more comfortable."

"Are they?" Corliss asked.

"Yes!" Patience replied.

"Well let me go find a pair then!" Corliss jumped from the table then trotted into the changing room. She returned in a pair of dungarees; her shirt tucked into the pants.

Sammy folded his arms. "You ain't going to stop this mess, Mama Bird?"

"No, I ain't," Mama Bird said.

Sammy shook his head. "Lord have mercy!"

They sat down to a good meal of fried chicken, corn on the cob and field peas. Corliss and Courtney dazzled everyone with their stories as they ate. The meal went faster than Patience expected, the time passing even faster. Sammy pushed away from the table, wiping his mouth with the napkin as he stood.

"We best be getting back to the station," he said. "That train will be rolling in soon."

"You don't want to miss it," Mama Bird said. "Someone's closer than you think."

Comfort drained from Patience's face replaced by worry. The images from the Missy's burning farm came to mind in morbid detail. She rushed to pack her things.

"Thanks for everything," Courtney said. "You going to be alright?"

Mama Bird smiled. "I'll be fine. He ain't worried about no small fish like me. Besides, the one thing he might want from me I gave to you."

Corliss grinned. "Knew there had to be a reason."

Patience returned and Mama Bird hugged her then kissed her cheek.

"Stay close to these two," she said. "They need you as much as you need them. They just don't know it yet."

"Yes ma'am," she replied. Patience had no idea what the twins needed from her, but she definitely needed them.

They followed Sammy to the wagon then climbed in. Sammy took them all the way to the train station, a single building with a single platform. The white people stood on the platform, looking down the tracks for the approaching train. The Negro riders gathered behind the station; their eyes focused on the same direction. The train whistle sound in the distance beyond the horizon. Ten minutes later locomotive arrived at the station then screeched to a stop. The people boarded; white passengers in the front seats, Negro passengers in the back back seats. Corliss, Courtney and Patience were about to board the first car when porter stepped between Courtney and Corliss.

"This car is full," he said. "You two will have to get on another car."

"But we're together," Courtney said.

"Doesn't matter," the porter replied. "We got enough Negroes in this car."

Courtney's eyes narrowed as he balled his fists.

"It's okay brother," Corliss said. "We're going to the same destination. You'll just get there a little sooner than us."

Courtney relaxed as he forced a smile on his face.

"See y'all in Atlanta," he said.

Courtney and Patience went to another car.

"Why did that porter separate us?" Patience asked. "There was plenty room."

"That's what white folks do," Corliss replied. "It don't matter. Things will be different in Nicodemus."

They boarded the last car, settled into their seats, and prepared for the long ride to Atlanta.

SIX

The swaying train rocked Patience to sleep. She dreamed of Trinidad again, of wide beaches trimmed by swaying palms, clear water filled with succulent fish and crustaceans, of lilting voices and fragrant spices, of long walks with Papa along the narrow cobblestone streets while munching on roti. The dream was so real Patience though she had somehow transported not only back home but back in time. She looked up to Papa and smiled.

"This is perfect," she said to him. "I want to stay here forever."

Papa looked down with a melancholy smile. *"That can't be, cheri. It's time for you to wake up. It's time for you to fight. Follow the bois."*

Patience opened her eyes just as Corliss reached for her.

"What is it?" she said.

"They caught up with us," Corliss said.

Patience looked out the train window. Small bright orbs of light danced outside, following the contours of the land as they edged closer and closer. Patience could make out the outlines despite the darkness. She immediately opened her box then took out the bois. The wood pulsed against her palms.

"What do we do?" she asked.

"We work our way to the engine and get the conductor to speed this damn thing up."

"How do we . . ."

A crashing sound broke Patience's words followed by screams. She jerked her head toward the sound to see a horrible sight; two hell hounds had jumped through the windows and were attacking the passengers. Without thinking she grabbed Corliss's arm then pulled her out of her seat.

"Girl, what are you doing?" Corliss shouted.

"Follow me!" she shouted. Patience ran up the narrow aisle, her bois lifted high. The hound closest to her dropped a ragged body from its maw and attacked her. Patience brought the bois down hard on its head, shattering its skull. She leaped over the lifeless body toward the second hound. The beast leaped as well. Patience gripped the bois like a cricket bat then swung with all her might. The stick cracked against the hound's head, sending spinning into and through a nearby window.

"Lord have mercy!" Corliss said.

Patience didn't stop to consider her newfound strength. She looked back toward Corliss, her face determined.

"Come on, Corliss," she said. "We got to save these folks!"

Corliss took out her machetes.

"I'm with you, girl!"

They rushed into the second car. The hounds had just begun their rampage, the passengers lucky enough to escape the initial attack fighting to leave the car. The hounds broke off their random killing as their targets entered. Five hounds attacked and Patience and Corliss made short work of them, hacking and beating the beasts to death. They met Courtney in the third car, his machetes a blur as he fought seven hounds. The passengers fled in every direction, some jumping out the windows to certain death. Patience knocked two hounds away from Courtney's legs as Corliss slipped by the big man to attack three hounds waiting for their turn to attack. Courtney dealt with the other two, grabbing them by the neck with his hand and throwing them from the train.

"Took y'all long enough," he said.

Patience looked down at his wounds

"Your legs! We need . . ."

"Don't have time for that," Courtney said. "We need to get to that engine."

They were crossing into the next car when something struck the train so hard, they fell against the bloody seats.

"What was that?" Patience yelled.

Courtney's face turned grim.

"Come on!"

Patience followed Courtney into the next car. Carnage awaited them. The hounds had apparently entered the train near the engine and worked their way to the rear car. Patience forced herself not to look at the mutilated passengers, focusing on Courtney's broad back. The train shook again, and they stumbled as they crossed into the final car. More ripped bodies greeted them, some still propped in their seats where they had been attacked without warning.

Courtney opened the final door. The coal cars rocked before them.

"We'll have to climb over them to reach the engine," Corliss shouted.

They were beginning to step out toward the car when Corliss spun about and pushed them back inside

"Hold onto something!" she shouted. "There's a curve coming and we're going too fast!"

Patience gripped a nearby seat, holding it as tight as she could. Courtney wrapped his arms around her and Corliss, forcing a smile to his face.

"Y'all ready?" he asked.

Patience was shaking her head as the train tilted. Courtney spun both she and Corliss around once he knew which way train would fall. There was a brief calm moment before the train smashed into the ground. Courtney grunted, his arms still tight around Patience and Corliss. Patience yelped as she was pelted with train debris. The train howled and shook as it slid across the ground to a hard stop. Courtney lost his grip and Patience tumbled across the train, bouncing off the seats then slamming against the door. She lay stunned for a moment then felt about for her bois. As she struggled to sit, her eyes found Courtney. He shook his head then pressed his finger against his lips.

Glass shattered and metal screeched in the distance. The sounds came closer. Patience fought back her fear as she listened. She managed to looked about and saw Corliss stirring in the far corner of the train. Courtney waved his arms trying to get her attention, but Corliss did not see him. Finally, he jumped up, stomping his feet.

"Over here!" he shouted.

No sooner did the words leave his lips did the windows above him shatter, showering him with glass. A massive snout plunged down; the mouth opened then closed around Courtney, yanking him from the train.

"No!" Corliss shouted. She ran then jumped through the hole after her brother.

"Go!" Patience heard her father say. *"Help them!"*

Patience climbed the seat then gingerly gripped the edges of the hole so not to cut her hands. She held her bois between her teeth as she emerged from the train. What she saw stunned her to stillness. An enormous hound held Courtney in its maw, Courtney struggling to break free. On its back was a figure holding the reins controlling the beast. Corliss was nearby, lifting her fiddle to her chest. She placed her bow on the strings then played a sound that struck the hound like a blow. It howled, dropping Courtney, and scrambling away.

"No, you don't!" the figure on its back shouted. "We almost got 'em! Get your ass back over there now!"

The hound gathered itself then charged toward Courtney. Courtney staggered to his feet. He yelled then ran at the hound, machetes in each hand. At the last second, he jumped, rising higher than Patience though any person could. Courtney somersaulted as he soared then landed on the hound's head before its rider. The huge man had a moment to look shocked before Courtney kicked him in the face and sent him tumbling to the ground. Courtney jumped off the hound's head, landing beside the man.

"Patience!" Corliss shouted.

Patience turned to look at Corliss who still played a discordant tune on her fiddle.

"Get between them," she shouted. "Courtney can't handle 'em both!"

Patience ran without thinking. The hound advanced toward Courtney as he fought the rider, the rider blocking Courtney's blades with his bare hands without being cut.

"Throw the bois," her papa said.

"But if I . . ."

"Throw the bois!" papa shouted.

Patience let the stick fly, stunned by the anger in papa's voice. He'd never yelled at her that way while he was alive. The stick streaked at the hound at a speed far beyond Patience's abilities, striking the hound in the jaw. The force was enough to turn the beast's head and send it careening left. Patience expected the bois to fall to the ground; instead in came back to her. He caught it in her right hand. She had little time to marvel, her father's voice shouted again.

"Throw it at the head!"

Patience stopped running, took aim then threw the bois. Once again it streaked with incredible speed toward the hound's ears. The beast turned toward Patience then emitted a blood churning howl. It managed to take two steps before the bois struck its head, breaking the forehead bones and embedding into the hound's skull. The devil dog collapsed immediately. Patience ran up to the foul beast then climbed onto its snout. She steadied herself then grasped the bois and pulled it free. She clambered down to the ground then set her eyes on the battle between Courtney and the giant brute. They exchanged blows like warring giants, both yelling and cursing as they struggled. Patience did not need papa's advice. She gripped the bois then ran toward the fray.

The hound rider's back was to her. She stopped running, tipping toward the man with the bois lifted over her head. Once she was close enough, she slashed down, striking the brute across his hamstrings. He yelled in pain then fell to his knees. As she raised the bois for a second strike the brute regained his feet then spun to face her.

"Black bitch!" he shouted.

Patience didn't see his hand move, but she felt it. The pain welling in her chest blinded her as she tumbled through the air then struck the ground. There was a sickening crack and then more pain. Patience lay on her back, each breath like a knife digging into her chest. The pain was so intense she couldn't keep her eyes open.

"Lord have mercy," she heard Corliss say.

Her body shifted as someone attempted to lift her. Pain shot through her torso.

"No!" she shouted.

"Damn girl, what you call yourself trying to do," Courtney said.

"We need to move her," Corliss said.

"Patience, I'm going to give you something for that pain," Courtney said.

"Oh . . . Okay," she said.

Something sweet touched her lips and she licked it instinctively. The pain in her chest eased.

"More," she said.

"A little bit more, but that's it," Courtney said. "Too much and you'll want it all the time."

Patience licked the paste as soon as it touched her lips. The pain disappeared and she was pulled into a deep sleep. She expected to see Papa while she slept but that was not to be. When she woke, she rested in darkness on a bed of leaves and straw. Courtney sat beside her, his arm in a makeshift sling, his clothes covered with blood. Corliss sat beside her and hummed a tune.

"Good to have you back among the living," she said.

Patience was about to sit up, but Corliss stopped her.

"Don't move. You got some broken bones. Courtney is working his roots on you but it's still gonna take some time."

"Yeah, you need to take it slow," Courtney said. "Old Cain gave you a good lick."

Patience strained to turn her head. "Cain? That demon has a name?"

"Had a name," Courtney said. "He ain't being called much of anything now except worm food."

"How do you know its name?" she asked.

"We'll talk about that later," Corliss said. "Right now, we need to get some food in you. Sip this."

Patience supped the warm broth. It was bitter but she felt the effects immediately. She took the bowl from Corliss and drank the concoction on her own. Corliss stood then put her hands on her hips.

"We look a mess," she said. "We're going to have to stay in one place for a while so y'all can heal."

"What about the demons?" Patience asked.

"We got some time," Courtney said. "Cain was one of Jedediah's best. He'll wait a spell before he sends anyone else."

"Jedediah?" Patience said. "Who's Jedediah?"

Courtney ignored her question.

"Don't have time or the strength to build a house," Corliss said. "We'll have to find something nearby to rent."

"You go on," Courtney said. "Me and Patience will be alright."

"You sure? I might be gone a few days."

"Do we have a choice? Go on now."

Corliss squatted beside Patience. "You try your best not to move. If I find a place for us to stay, I'll see if I can get a wagon for you."

"Thank you," Patience said.

"You still here?" Courtney asked.

Corliss glared at Courtney. "I'm going."

She patted Patience's shoulder.

"Keep an eye on Courtney," she said as she winked.

With that she stood then walked away, following the railroad tracks west. Patience shifted and pain flared in her chest. The broth seemed only to work as long as she remained still.

Courtney came over to her then sat. He took his arm from the sling and moved it about, wincing as he worked it up and down.

"That damned Cain," he said. "Always was a tough one."

"You've fought him before?" Patience asked.

"Yeah."

"You knew him?"

Courtney sighed. "I know every haint, ghoul and ghost that works for Jedediah. Every last one of them."

"How?"

"'Cause I used to be one of them. Me and Corliss both."

Terror hit Patience. She wanted to run but knew she couldn't. Instead, she looked at Courtney helplessly. He read her expressed then frowned.

"I said used to. We broke up that arrangement a long time ago. Jedediah's been after us ever since."

"Why did you leave him?" Patience asked.

"You see what he's done. You need to ask that question?"

"But you served him before. Why?"

Courtney shifted. "Because he made us."

"Made you?"

Courtney nodded. "He took a handful of marsh mud and sweetgrass, molded our forms then breathed life into us. Then he gave us our talents. Made me strong and good with roots, made Corliss fast with machetes and magic in her voice. We did whatever he told us to do until the day we met Missy."

"But you told me you grew up on a farm," Patience said.

"Some part of us did," Courtney replied. "We have memories of things that happened to us, but they didn't. Seeing how we was conceived, they couldn't have. Don't know where they came from and I'm scared to find out."

Patience tried to roll onto her side, forgetting her injury. She winced then rolled back onto her back.

"How did Missy change you?"

"Jedediah sent us to kill her," Courtney said. "Wasn't the first time we were sent to do so. When we arrived, she was sitting on her porch smoking a pipe. She knew why we were there; we could feel it. Usually when that happened, folks would either run or fight, which made what we had to do easy. But she just sat there."

Courtney got a faraway look in his eyes.

"When we got to her porch, she took that pipe out of her mouth, stared at both of us and said, 'What y'all waiting for? Let's get this over with."

"That caught us off guard," Courtney said. "All that time serving Jedediah and we ain't never come across anybody that wasn't afraid of him. She knew it too. She just looked at us and smiled."

"Y'all wonder why I ain't scared," she said. "It's because I know that when y'all do what y'all about to do I still got living to do. You ain't nothing but mud and grass. Nothing but mud and grass."

Courtney rubbed his sore arm. "It was something about the way she said it. I ain't ever thought about the future before then. She might have worked some kind of roots on us, I don't know. Whatever she did, it worked. We been on our own ever since."

"So, you don't work with Miss Harriett?"

Courtney shook his head. "I wouldn't know that woman if she walked up to me and bit me on the ankle. We're doing this on our own . . . and for Missy."

Courtney leaned against the tree.

"Enough talking," he said. "You need to rest. The more you rest the faster you heal."

"You too," Patience said.

"I'll be alright. You forgot what I am."

"Who you are," Patience corrected.

Courtney grinned. "That's right. Who I am."

Patience fell asleep then entered the presence of her father. He was dressed immaculately in white pants and shirt, a pair of sandals on his feet. He smiled at her and Patience smiled back. She rushed to hug him, savoring his presence even though she knew he was dead.

"You did well," he said.

"I didn't do anything," she replied. It was you . . . and the ancestors."

"The techniques were new to you, but it was your skill and strength that performed the action."

"I've never made a bois fly and return," Patience said. "Never."

"There are many things the bois can do," Papa said. *"If you can imagine it, it can do it. It can achieve almost anything you think it can."*

"Can it bring you back?"

"No."

They were silent for a moment, Patience refusing to let Papa go. As she held him, he faded away and Patience slept.

SEVEN

Patience woke to the creaking of an approaching wagon. She lifted her head, remembering not to lift her body. Courtney was on his feet, shielding his eyes as he looked toward the direction of the sound.

"Took you long enough," he said.

"Next time you go," Corliss replied. "I'd be happy to stay behind for some peace and quiet."

A middle-aged Negro man stepped from behind Corliss, his thick lips twisted into a frown.

"These here your kinfolk?" he asked.

"Yes, suh," Corliss answered. "My brother and my sister. My sister is the one who's hurt."

The man shuffled over to Patience, studying her as if he could do something for her.

"Come on, boy," he said to Courtney. "Let's get her in the wagon."

Courtney knelt on the right side of Patience, the man on her left. They slipped their hands underneath her and she braced for the pain about to occur.

"Be careful now!" Corliss blurted.

"It's gonna hurt no matter how careful we are," the man said. "Let's get this over quick."

They jerked her up and Patience screamed. They set her down just as suddenly and Patience almost passed out.

The man looked down on her.

"That was the easy part," he said. "The ride back is going to be worse."

It was. Every bump and jostle sent searing flashes throughout her body. Corliss sat beside her, stroking her hair and singing, but even her hypnotic voice couldn't cancel out the pain. When the wagon finally stopped Patience thanked God. The pain of them lifting her and taking her inside the small house was nothing in comparison. They set her down on something soft.

"Here you go," Corliss said. "Three months' rent up front."

"Well is out back,' the man said. "You free to use it. I expect y'all can find work in Dublin. Lots of folks around here need good farmhands, and a couple of the white folks wouldn't mine you working in their houses, especially being as pretty as you are. My wife can watch over your little sister here until she's better."

"Thank you kindly, Mr. Wade," Corliss said. "I know you need to be getting on now."

"Yes, I do."

Mr. Wade shuffled out of the house, climbed into his wagon and rode away. No sooner had he left did Courtney slam his fist on the small table before the fireplace.

"Three months!" We can't stay here for three months!"

"Well, we're gonna to have to," Corliss replied. "It's going to take Patience at least that long to heal, and I just gave Mr. Wade our last bit of money."

"I was about to get to that," Courtney said.

"We don't need the money," Corliss said. "We can make do without it. Besides, we know how to get it when we need it. The most important thing is Patience. I know you're worried about Jedediah catching up with us but killing Cain and his hounds is going to slow things down a bit. I'm suspecting old Scratch is a little confused right about now."

"Probably rubbing that bald head of his wondering what the hell is going on," Courtney replied.

Corliss hunched over then scrunched up her face. She pulled at her chin as if she had a beard.

"Now where da hell is Cain?" she said in a deep voice. "Dat fool shoulda been done kilt dem troublemakers and dat little gal!"

Courtney assumed the same posture.

"And where is my puppies? Hey puppies! Hey puppies! Where y'all at?"

He shuffled around the small house, looking behind the dusty furniture and under the table. Patience laughed then winced.

"Please stop!" she said. "It hurts when I laugh."

Courtney bolted up straight then pointed at Patience.

"Dere my puppy!" he shuffled over to Patience then kissed her on the forehead.

"Courtney!" Corliss exclaimed.

But it was too late. The pain in Patience's chest became unbearable. She screamed, hoping that it would end, willing to do anything to make it stop. She thrashed about on the bed, trying to shake the agony from her body. Courtney held her down.

"I'm sorry Patience. I'm sorry!" he said.

Corliss joined him, adding her strength.

"It will be over in a minute," she said with her soothing voice. "The less you fight, the less it will hurt."

Patience couldn't hear them. She was no longer in the small house. She streaked across a liquid blackness, the pain diminishing into a pulsing pressure. The blackness shifted into an unfamiliar landscape. Her feet touched ground; she looked about to see a land like which she'd never seen before. A large figure lumbered toward her, changing appearance with every step.

"I got you now," it said. "Courtney and Corliss still belong to me no matter what they do."

The figure reached out toward her. Patience tried to back away but her feet were cemented to the ground. The thing was about to grab her when the blackness swallowed her again. When she opened her eyes Corliss and

Courtney hovered over her, their faces etched with fatigue.

"She's back," Corliss said. "We brought her back!"

Courtney didn't say anything. He slumped to the floor, covering his face with his hands.

"We're so glad your back," Corliss said in her sweet voice. Patience drew away.

"Stay away from me," she said. "Stay away."

Corliss took her hand away. "Listen honey, things are a bit complicated. We don't serve Jedediah no more, but he still has a hold on us. I know you're scared, but trust us. If we meant you harm, your daddy would have told you."

Patience looked at both of them with a different eye. Jedediah would always know where she was as long as she was with them. Yet she didn't know the way to Nicodemus on her own. But would it make a difference if she made the journey?

"I want to go home," she finally said. "I want to go back to Trinidad. You can have papa's bois. That's what you really want. That's what Jedediah wants."

"Stop talking crazy!" Courtney said. Corliss cut him a mean eye.

"Peanut, now ain't the time for you to lose your temper."

"Hush up, Corliss," he said. "I'm talking to Patience."

Courtney stared at Patience which made her more fearful.

"Do you think we wanted to do this?" he said. "Do you think we volunteered? Hell naw! We did this because Missy said it was important. Now we put up with you so far, but we ain't doing it no more. You got half a chance of staying alive with us but you ain't got no chance without us. So, make up your mind what you want to do. But I can tell you one thing, you won't make it five miles let alone all the way back to Trinidad or wherever the hell you came from without us!"

Patience scrambled off the bed to her box, ignoring her pain the best she could. She gathered her things then went to the door.

"Patience, don't," Corliss said.

"I'd rather be dead than be with both of you," she said. "At least I'd be with my mama and papa!"

She opened the door ran into the darkness. She had the barest plan in mind and she hoped it would work. If she could find the railroad tracks, she would follow them back to Savannah. Once she returned, she would figure out a way to get back to Trinidad. As she walked deeper into the darkness, she looked over her shoulder to see if she was being followed. There was no movement in the cabin; no one followed her. She should have been happy but she wasn't. She was truly alone.

"I'll be okay," she said aloud. "Jedediah doesn't want me or papa's bois. He just doesn't want me to go to Nicodemus, so I won't."

The darkness became an obstacle as she reached a stand of oak trees bordering a narrow creek. She cleared a space under a clump of bushes then tried to sleep the best she could. She was about to doze off when she realized the pain in her chest was gone. She sat up, feeling her body as if she could decipher her health. She thought about Courtney's kiss then shuddered. It seemed his contact healed her. If that was so, why hadn't he done it sooner? Because he knew what the contact would do. Was he trying to protect her? She was too tired to decide. She placed her head on her bundle and finally fell into a dreamless frightful sleep.

EIGHT

A bright sun and a horde of voracious mosquitoes snapped Patience from sleep. She swiped at the annoying insects as she stood and gathered her bag and bois. Her stomach growled, so she opened her back and ate one of the hard biscuits she'd taken from the cabin. It tasted terrible but it was all she had. She washed down the biscuit with a couple of handfuls of creek water then walked to the tracks and began her journey back to Savannah. She had no idea how long they traveled on the train, but she knew that somewhere along the way she would come to a small town where she could rest and find more to eat. The reality was she had no idea what she was doing. She'd never been on her own and she was terrified. But it was either go back to Savannah alone or stay with the twins.

By afternoon she was tired and hungry with no sign of a house or town in sight. She opened her bag and sighed; he had half a biscuit left. She took a small bite then continued following the tracks. It was almost nightfall when she finally had reason to hope. She saw a home in the distance surrounded by fields of some kind of vegetable. She staggered toward the home, not caring whether Negro or white people lived there. She just wanted water and food.

Patience was hurrying toward the porch when she heard the growl. She dropped her bags then took papa's bois from its case. A German Shepherd ran from around the house, its teeth bared. Patience raised her bois to strike if the dog came any closer.

"Saber! Stop!"

The dog pulled up just short of Patience, a hair out of distance of her bois. A woman ran from the house, jumping down the stairs then kneeling by the dog. She looked up at Patience with an angry look on her young face.

"You weren't planning on hitting him with that, were you?" the woman said.

"Yes I was," Patience said. "He was about to bite me."

"He was doing his job," the woman said. "You're trespassing."

"I'll drop my bois if you promise he won't bite me."

"Your what?"

"My bois . . . I mean my stick," Patience said.

"Gone on back, Saber," the woman said. "Go on back now."

She let the dog go and it trotted back around the house, barking a few times as it walked away.

"He's well trained," Patience said as she lowered her bois.

"Who are you?" the woman asked. "And what are you doing way out here by yourself? You ain't one of them Gypsies, are you?"

"My name is Patience and I'm not a Gypsy," Patience said. "I'm just trying to get back to Savannah. I fell in with some people who turned out not to be what they said they were."

The woman's expression softened. "I know what that feels like."

She looked at the house then back to Patience.

"You hungry?" she asked.

"Very," Patience replied.

The woman extended her hand. "I'm Betsy Hammond. I got dinner on the stove if you'd like some."

Patience shook the woman's hand.

"Nice to meet you, Miss Betsy. And I would like some."

"Okay. And it's just Betsy. I ain't too much older than you."

Patience followed Betsy into the house. It was a modest dwelling, a two-room home neatly kept. Beside the small bed was a cradle.

"You have a baby?" Patience asked.

"Uh huh" Betsy replied. "A baby girl. Her name is Rose."

"Can I see her?" Patience asked.

"Go ahead. Don't pick her up. I just put her to sleep."

Patience tipped to the cradle. Rose slept soundly, her small chest rising and falling. She was a beautiful child, too young to tell if she resembled her mother.

When Patience turned back Betsy was preparing a plate for her.

"Where is your husband?" she asked.

"He went into town for supplies," Betsy said. "He's supposed to catch the train back. He should have come back yesterday."

A chill swept through Patience. Was her husband on their train? If so, it was a good chance he would never return.

"Your plate is ready," Betsy said.

Patience sat down to a full plate of corn, collards, and snap beans. Betsy sat before her; Patience was about to start eating before Betsy shook her head.

"Got to say grace first," Betsy said.

"Of course," Patience replied. She bowed her head then took Betsy's hands.

"Dear Lord, thank you for the food we are about to receive. Bless the cook and thank you for the company. In Jesus name we pray, Amen."

"Amen," Patience said. She let go of Betsy's hands, scooped up a forkful of corn then stuffed it in her mouth.

"Looks like your pretty hungry," Betsy commented.

"It's been two days since I had a full meal," Patience replied. "Thank you so much."

"You still haven't told me how you came to be out here."

Patience chewed slowly as she decided how much to share with Betsy. She knew she wouldn't believe the truth, yet she didn't want to lie to someone who shared her home and food.

"I'm from Trinidad," she began. "Me and my papa were coming to America to visit an old friend of his in Nicodemus, Kansas. There was a fire our ship. My father was caught in the flames and died."

"Lord Jesus," Betsy said. "I'm so sorry."

"It's okay," Patience said. He's still with me . . . inside."

Patience touched her chest.

"I understand. But how did you get way out here?"

"When I arrived in Savannah there was a man waiting for me and papa. He took me to Missy, who told me she would get me to Nicodemus. She introduced me to the two people who I traveled with until I realized they were not what they told me they were. So, I left them."

Betsy nodded. "Uh huh. Why didn't you just wait and catch the train?"

"Because I thought they would try to stop me."

"But they didn't."

Patience played with her corn. "No, they didn't."

"Well, it sounds like a bad situation," Betsy said. "But it's alright. You're here now. When my husband gets back, he'll take you to the station so you can get a train back to

Savannah. I would take you, but I have to watch the baby."

"I don't have money for the train," Patience admitted.

"That's alright," Betsy said. "I have a few dollars stashed away."

"You don't have to do that," Patience said. "I'll manage."

"No, you won't," Betsy said. "How old are you, thirteen?"

"Twelve," Patience said.

"Too young to be traipsing about on your own. I wouldn't be able to live with myself if I let you walk out of this house alone. I just wouldn't."

"You are so kind," Patience said.

"Aw shush now," Betsy replied. "I'm sure you'd do the same for me. Now let's finish this supper then get you to bed."

A weak cry interrupted them.

"Excuse me," Betsy said. "Feeding time."

She ate another forkful of collards before going to her child.

"Mama's coming, baby!" she called out.

Patience finished her meal then took her plate to the sink. She washed it clean then went to Betsy, who was feeding the child.

"You done with your supper?" she asked.

"I might as well be," Betsy replied.

"I'll finish the dishes for you."

Betsy smiled. "You don't have to, sugar. I'll be done directly."

Patience shook her head. "It's the least I can do."

"Well bless your heart," Betsy said. "You are a sweet one."

"I'm grateful," Patience said. "Let me know what else you need done."

Patience pumped water into the sink then washed the dishes. She hummed papa's song as she washed, letting her guard down for the first time in days. As she stacked the last dish Betsy entered the kitchen.

"What a good job!" she said. "It's so nice to have a helping hand around the house. My husband is not much help inside, even when he's here."

"Thank you," Patience said. "Is there somewhere I can wash up?"

"I have a wash bin in the baby's room. I'll bring it out. I'll go back inside the room if you need some privacy. We can wash those clothes tomorrow."

"I wasn't planning on being here that long," Patience said. "I don't want to bring no trouble."

"You ain't no trouble at all, Patience," Betsy said.

Betsy went into the baby's room then returned with the wash bin, two towels and a bar of lye soap. Patience washed down the best she could, happy to feel at least partially clean. Betsy's timing was perfect again.

"I'll throw the water out for you," she said. "Go on and lay down. I know you're tired."

"Yes, ma'am I am," Patience said.

"I hope you don't mind us sharing a bed," Betsy said.

"Not really," Patience said.

She went to the bed and lay down. No sooner did her head touch the pillow did she fall asleep. Just as suddenly she found herself standing in front of Papa.

"Patience, where are you?" he asked, his voice filled with urgency.

"I'm in a house with a woman name Betsy," she answered. "I left Courtney and Corliss. I'm going back to Trinidad."

"That was a foolish thing to do," Papa said. *"You must return to them now."*

"I can't papa," she replied. "They are not who you think they are. They used to serve Jedediah."

"I know," Papa said.

Patience was shocked. "You knew?"

"Yes," Papa said. *"Who else could better protect you than those that once served him? Every moment you are away from them the more danger you are in. Wake up now!"*

Patience's eye snapped open. Standing over her holding a kerosene lantern was Betsy.

"What's the matter Patience?" she asked. "Did you have a bad dream?"

Patience sat up, reaching instinctively for her bois case. It was gone.

"Are you looking for this?"

Betsy lifted her left hand, bringing papa's bois case into view.

"Give that back," Patience said. "It's mine."

"You don't need it," Betsy said. "You're safe here. You don't have to worry about those people who tricked you. Once my husband returns, he'll make sure you'll be safe from now on."

Patience concentrated to keep herself from shaking. She would not panic. She looked about the house, trying to figure out some way to escape. It was then she noticed there were no windows to the small house.

"Lie back down and get some rest," Betsy said. "In the morning we'll make breakfast and take turns watching the baby. It will be fun; I promise."

"I would sleep better if I had my bois," Patience said.

"I told you, you don't need it. I have everything under control."

Betsy's eyes narrowed as she smiled. Patience lay back down then pretended to sleep until Betsy walked away. She opened her eyes hoping to see her bois case nearby but it was nowhere in sight. She sighed, resigned to whatever would come in the morning. What worried her most was Betsy's husband. Who was he? Was he the man she saw in her dream, the man she thought was Jedediah? She shook her head to clear her thoughts. Deal with the problem in front of you, not the one ahead of you, papa always said.

Patience tried to sleep that night but her fear wouldn't let her. She would close her eyes when she heard Betsy approaching; opening them when she was sure the woman was gone. Then she would search the house again for some way out. The door she'd entered through no longer existed, neither did the windows. She was a prisoner with no way out.

To her surprise Patience awoke to sunlight. The windows had reappeared as had the door. She sat up, dressed then walked into the kitchen space. Betsy was cooking over the iron stove humming an unfamiliar song. The baby's crib was in its room nearby, shaking now and then as the little one moved about. Sitting at the table was a large man, his head completely bald. The man turned then looked at Patience. Patience shuddered when she saw his face; his pupils were slit like a cat's and his smile revealed his sharp canines.

"Patience, you're awake!" Betsy said. "Sit down and have some breakfast."

Betsy brought two plates to the table. She sat one before the big man and one on the table where Patience assumed she would sit.

"Patience, I'd like you to meet my husband, Malcolm Turner."

Patience nodded as she sat at the table before her plate. As she sat, she saw a sight that gave her hope; the bois case propped in a kitchen corner.

"It's good to meet you Patience," he said. His voice was deep and gravely. "Betsy tells me you're lost."

They talked as if everything was normal, as if she didn't know what was happening. They were holding her until Jedediah arrived then they would give her to him.

"I'm not lost," she finally said. "I'm heading to Savannah."

"Savannah? You mean Savannah, Georgia? Gal, do you realize how far you're away from Savannah?"

"I'll make it if you'll let me," she said.

"We're not stopping you, honey," Betsy said. "We have a friend that will make sure you get back. He knows the way very well."

Patience pushed her plate away then stood.

"If you don't mind, I'll leave now," she said.

"Finish your breakfast," Betsy said. "Our friend is on his way."

"No," Patience said. "Let me out. Now."

"You might as well sit down and eat girl," Malcolm said. "You ain't going anywhere until it's time."

Patience decided at that point she had nothing to lose. She pretended to sit then sprinted toward her bois box. Betsy sprang toward her, her arms outstretched. Patience stopped long enough to kick the woman in the stomach so hard she doubled over.

"God damn it!" she wheezed.

Patience was almost to the box when Malcolm appeared, blocking her way with his massive body.

"Now why did you have to go do that?" he said. "Betsy was on her best behavior. She thought she could win you over. Looks like I'm going to have to let her do it another way."

Malcolm's open palm smashed against the side of Patience's head, knocking her into the wall. She rolled into the baby's room.

"Get her out of there before it's too late!" Malcolm yelled.

"Let it have her!" Betsy shouted back.

"You want to answer to Jedediah? I sure as hell don't!"

Patience felt a hand grip her ankle. She was dragged from the room back into the kitchen. She heard a door slam.

"What do we do with her until then?" Betsy asked.

"Tie her up and wait," Malcolm answered. "We got the stick now. All we have to do is . . ."

The entire house shook, plates and pots rattling in the cupboard.

"Is Jedediah here already?" Betsy asked.

"That ain't Jedediah," Malcolm said.

Patience sat up to look at her captives. They stood in the center of the kitchen, looking to and fro.

"What the hell is it then?" Betsy asked.

Malcolm grimaced. "It's the twins. They done come for her."

A familiar discordant sound penetrated the walls. Malcolm and Betsy winced as a gruesome howl came from the 'baby's' room. The sound grew louder and Malcolm and Betsy bodies contorted. As they changed fear took hold of Patience.

"No. No!" she screamed.

They transformed into the same creatures Patience saw that night in papa's room, monsters of flesh and fire. The house shook again, and the walls splintered near the door.

"Stop him!" Betsy shouted.

Malcolm ran to the fractured wall section and braced it with his weight. Oddly, the wood did not burn with his touch. A familiar arm punched through the wall then clamped around Malcolm head, pinning him to the wall.

"Help me!" he shouted.

As Betsy scrambled to help Malcolm, Patience ran to her bois case then took out papa's bois. His voice filled her head as soon as her hands wrapped around the smooth wood.

"Help them!" he said.

Patience hesitated. She looked on as Betsy wrapped her fiery fingers around Courtney's forearm and yanked it.

"If you don't help them, they cannot save you," Papa said.

Patience relented. She held the bois high as she rushed then brought it down hard on Betsy's head. Flames exploded toward her face and she staggered back. When her eyes cleared Betsy was turned toward her in full flames.

"Bitch!" she yelled.

She was about to attack when a loud cracking sound came from behind her. Malcolm howled as Courtney pulled him through the wall. Betsy ran after him; Patience was close behind. She was jumping through the hole when something grabbed her leg and pulled her back. Patience fell but didn't lose her bois; she turned onto her back to see an alligator-like creature with tentacles slithering across the floor toward her. One of the tentacles gripped her right ankle. Patience screamed as the creature slid closer, its tooth-filled jaws snapping. She couldn't hit the tentacle without striking her ankle as well.

"Wait," Papa said.

"It will eat me!" she exclaimed.

"No, wait," he said. *"Its head is a much bigger target."*

Patience waited, using every ounce of her control not to panic. When the creature was almost to her foot it reared then let loose a gurgled cry before lunging at her.

"Now!" Papa said.

Patience gripped the base of the bois and swung with all her might. The stick smacked the beast's jaws, knocking its head to the side. Its grip loosened on her ankle. Patience struck it again; this time she was rewarded with a sickening crack. The beast's mouth fell open, its jaw shattered. It let go of her ankle as it howled and thrashed its head about, throwing spittle and blood throughout the room. She clambered to her feet then ran for the opening torn into the wall by

Courtney. The floor under her feet buckled as the creature gathered itself and pursued her despite its damaged mouth. As she reached the opening Courtney blocked it, a bloody machete raised over his head and a scowl on his face.

"Get down!" he shouted.

Patience fell to the floor as Courtney threw the machete. The weapon plunged into the croc-beast's mouth then tore through its head. The blade stuck into the opposite wall. He glared at her as he strode by, stepped over the dead creature then pulled his machete out of the wall. On his way back to the wall he grabbed Patience's arm, pulled her to her feet then dragged her from the house.

"What about the baby?" Patience said.

Courtney stopped the pointed his machete at the dead alligator-beast.

"That was the baby," he said.

Patience gained her footing as they walked through the Courtney's hole. The monster that was Betsy lay on the porch; her head attached to her body by a sliver of skin. Malcolm lay a few feet away, his body twisted in odd angles. Corliss stopped playing then ran to them, a relieved smile on her face.

"Thank the Lord you're alright!" she said.

"Corliss, Courtney, I'm sorry. I . . ."

A piercing howl interrupted Patience's apology.

"Damned hellhounds! Courtney said.

"How many?" Corliss asked.

Courtney looked into the distance the frowned.

"Too many," he said.

"I know a place we can make a stand," Corliss said. "I felt it on the way here."

"Well let's get going!" Courtney said.

They ran. Patience ran as fast as she could but couldn't keep up. They sprinted across the fields then into the nearby woods, the twins darting between the trees like they possessed another set of eyes for the dark, the distance between them and her increasing with every step. Behind her the death hounds paced themselves. She knew they could rush her at any moment, take her down then tear her apart. She gripped her bois tight, read to fight off any hound that dared come close. But her bravery waned as the baying hounds came closer.

She ran into something hard then fell on her backside. She raised her bois, ready for the attack.

"Damn you slow, girl," Courtney said. "Get on!"

Courtney turned his back to her then squatted. Patience hesitated.

"Come on now girl. Hurry up!"

Patience climbed onto Courtney's back. He ran full out, carrying Patience like she was a feather in his pocket. In moments he ran alongside Corliss.

"You find 'em yet?" he said, his voice shaky.

"No," Corliss answered.

"Maybe there ain't none," Courtney said.

"They're here somewhere," Corliss said. "We down South. Can't take ten steps without finding them."

They emerged into a field of wiregrass illuminated by the full moon. The death hounds followed them into the muted light, their hoarse barking echoing across the expanse. Halfway across the field Corliss stopped then took out her fiddle. The hounds showed themselves, their eyes flickering like small flames.

"Right here!" she said.

She played, her first note, a low sound Patience could barely hear. The hounds heard it, stopping as they thrashed their heads in obvious pain. Once the dogs stood still, she switched to a melancholy song that pulled forth memories of her father from Patience's mind. She dropped her bois then covered her tearful eyes.

Courtney picked up the bois then handed it back to her. He pulled her close.

"Stay close. It's just getting started."

The ground shook. Patience held Courtney tighter as mounds of dirt rose around them then burst open. She held back a scream as malformed bodies emerged from the grass, misshapen shapes draped in dilapidated blue and gray uniforms. Corliss continued playing as the bodies formed a circle around them.

"What . . . what are they?" she said.

"They used to be soldiers," Courtney said. "Johnny Rebs and Yankees. Now they gonna be our protection, at least until I have to put 'em back down."

"Put them down?"

Patience looked at Courtney with questioning eyes.

"You'll see," he said. His voice was not happy.

The hounds attacked and the undead warriors responded. A macabre battle took place around them as Corliss continued to play, sweat pooling under her arms and running down her face. The skeletal warriors pranced like puppets, cutting the hounds apart with their jagged bones.

"Get ready Courtney!" she shouted. "Them soldiers about done doing our work for us!"

Courtney let go of Patience. He opened the pouch on his waist then extracted a small leather bag. Corliss continued to play as she backed toward Courtney and Patience.

The dead soldiers ripped the hounds apart. As the last dog was torn to pieces, the undead army turned its attention to them.

"Y'all get down!" Courtney said. Corliss dropped to a crouch; Patience stood wide eyed staring at the approaching soldiers.

"Get down here, girl!" Corliss shouted. "You deaf?"

Patience eased down beside the scowling woman. Courtney brought the pouch to his lips then chanted; his words muffled by the bag. The soldiers dragged closer, their stench forcing Patience to hold her nose. She heard the rattling bones, the half-covered feet swishing over the bent grass.

"Courtney!" she blurted.

"Hush up girl!" Corliss said. "He knows what he's doing."

The dead soldiers were almost upon them when Courtney opened pouch then poured the contents into his hand. He took a deep breath then blew the gray power onto the soldiers, turning slowly as the dust wafted over the soldiers. His concoction slowed the soldiers, but didn't stop them.

"Y'all helping?" he said.

He smashed the flat of his blade against the nearest cadaver. The soldier crumbled into a pile of dust that seeped into the ground. Corliss joined him, putting her fiddle back into her shoulder case then taking her machetes from her back sheaths.

"You must help them," Baba said in Patience's head.

"I'm afraid," she answered.

"Don't be. The danger is over. They helped you now you must help them."

"What do I do?" she said.

"Hold the bois over your head," baba said. *"Close your eyes, then call on the ancestors."*

The cadavers converged as Patience raised the bois over her head as baba instructed.

"Gal! what are you doing?" Courtney shouted. "We need your help!"

"Leave her alone!" Corliss yelled. "She's about to give it to us!"

"Ancestors," Patience said. "Please help us."

As the last words escaped her lips Patience was swept with a rush from her feet to her head. Her braid blew wild as if she stood in the middle of a storm.

"We are coming . . . we are coming . . . we are coming!"

Patience went rigid. The bois quaked in her hands, then heat exploded from it like a desert wind. Spectral shapes of men and women burst from the bois, a spiritual wave flooding in every direction. Each spirit wielded a bois, which it used to beat down the undead soldiers swarming around them. For the first time since they had been summoned, an expression came to the dead warriors' ruined faces; fear. They cowered as the spirits set upon them; some even attempted to run away. Courtney kept battling the dead; Corliss sheathed her machetes and took out her fiddle. She played a sweet melody that seemed to increase the vigor of the rescuing spirits. The spirits continued their onslaught until all the undead warriors were a layer of gray dust on the grass. Then they swirled to the rhythm of Corliss's music, a divine dance in celebration of their victory. Corliss slowed the pace and the spirits returned to the bois. Patience felt her body come under her control again. She lowered her arms, then looked at Corliss and Courtney.

"Well, I'll be damned," Courtney said. "I ain't never seen anything like that in my entire life."

"Me neither," Corliss replied.

Patience sat hard on the grass, totally exhausted. Courtney sat beside her; his arms stretched behind him. Corliss ambled to them then sat down opposite Patience. Courtney looked at her then grinned. He reached out and tossed her braids about.

"You did mighty fine, gal. Mighty fine," he said.

Corliss smiled at her. "Told you she was gonna be alright."

Patience didn't smile back.

"I was scared," she said. "But Papa told me to be strong."

She clutched the bois against her chest.

"The spirits will do that," Courtney said. "They give us strength when we weak."

Corliss buckled the straps to her fiddle case then stood.

"Let's get out of this graveyard," she said. "We'll camp over there a ways then set out in the morning. Maybe we can hop a train to the next town."

"I hope so," Courtney said. He took off his shoes then began rubbing his feet. "These dogs are starting bark."

"Please don't say dogs," Patience said.

Corliss and Courtney laughed.

"Told you she was gonna be alright," Corliss said.

NINE

Patience, Courtney and Corliss trudged through the woods, Corliss leading the way. Patience looked at the twins pensively. She fled thinking they meant her harm and they came and save her life. After they set up camp, Courtney found a soft spot then fell to sleep. Corliss fussed about, inspecting her fiddle then taking Courtney's machetes. She sang low as she cleaned, sharpened and oiled the blades then put them back into their sheaths. She did the same to her own machetes, humming while she labored. Patience watched her as she hugged her knees against her chest. She waited until Corliss was about to lie down before she stood and approached her.

"Corliss?" she said.

Corliss looked up then smiled. "What you want, baby?"

Patience tipped over to Corliss then knelt beside her.

"I want to say thank you for coming for me. I'm sorry for not trusting you and Courtney."

The weight of the day finally crashed down on her and she cried. She felt Corliss's arms wrap around her then pull her tight.

"It's okay, baby,' she said. "You had reason to doubt us. I wanted to come after you as soon as you ran away but Courtney was madder than a fox on fire. Took me three days to calm him down. You don't have to apologize to me, but you might want to say a word or two to him once he wakes up."

Patience wiped her eyes.

"I will."

Corliss smiled. "Good. Now get some sleep. We have a long walk ahead of us."

Patience retired to a spot close to Courtney. She wanted to be nearby when he woke so she could apologize first thing in the morning. She fell asleep quickly and just as suddenly found herself sitting before Papa in the center of a field of wildflowers. Papa smiled at her the way he did when she'd done well.

"The ancestors are pleased," he said. *"You fought well."*

"I was afraid," she said. "I'm not a very good warrior."

"All warriors are afraid when they go into battle," he said. *"If they're not then they are fools. The key is that you did not let your fear control you. You overcame it and fought. You didn't let your friends down."*

"They are my friends, aren't they?" she said.

"Yes, they are," Papa replied. *"They would die for you."*

"Why?" she asked. "They barely know me."

"They will die for you because they know who you will become. Jedediah knows, too."

"Everyone speaks of what I am to be," she said. "When will I know?"

"Miss Tubman will tell you," Papa said. *"For now, get some sleep. It is a long journey ahead."*

Patience let go of papa's image and quickly fell into a deep slumber. The sun was warm on her face when she awoke. Courtney stirred near her, his massive body rising and falling with his breath. Patience moved closer to him.

"Courtney?"

Courtney sat up and rubbed his eyes.

"What?"

Patience touched his shoulder.

"I'm sorry."

Courtney turned and looked her directly in the eyes.

"About what?"

"About leaving . . . and not trusting you."

Courtney shrugged. "You're back now. That's all that matters. We had to backtrack a bit, but we'll make up the time. We're about a day's walk from the next station. We should be alright between here and Nicodemus."

"What about Jedediah?" Patience asked.

"We gave him a good whupping back there," Courtney said. "It's going to be a while before he takes a lick at us again."

Courtney stretched then stood.

"Guess we better get a move on."

They made good time over the next few days, sticking close to the roads when possible and following the tracks when the woods became too difficult. Patience made up for her earlier doubt by being very attentive to everything the twins shared. She became a decent hunter and learned to clean and cook wild game despite her earlier aversion. When food was scarce, they would find a local town or cluster of homes and perform. Sometimes they were paid in money; other times they were given food and a place to sleep for the night. All the while Patience looked back, hoping she would not see the face of Jedediah smiling back at her. Courtney said they had nothing to worry about for a while, but Patience had no idea what a while meant. Would it be three days, a month, six months? In her dreams, papa told her not to worry, but in her waking mind worry was all she could do.

She also practiced. Courtney was not good with the bois but he was excellent with machetes and a formidable opponent. He was careful to use the flat of his blades, pushing her much harder than papa ever did. He cut her a few times, whether by accident or on purpose Patience wasn't sure. Whatever the reason, it made her more diligent. The reason she trained so much was that it was the only time papa visited her during the day. He would comment on her every move, telling her when a better technique presented itself and scolding her when she made a bad mistake. Gradually his comments diminished. Patience began penetrating Courtney's defenses, landing a few blows here and there. The frowns on Courtney's face when she struck him became her reward and her goal. They became so frequent that their sessions ended sooner so Courtney could treat his wounds. Corliss watched it all, cheering Patience on.

"Whup his ass!" she shouted.

"You're my sister," Courtney fussed. "You're supposed to be on my side!"

"As much hell you raise, it's about time somebody gave you a bit a grief," Corliss said.

"Why don't you play a bad song or something?" he said. "Ouch!"

Patience struck Courtney at the elbow. He winced as he dropped his machete.

"That was my funny bone!" he yelped.

"Did it feel funny?" Patience asked.

Courtney burst out laughing.

"Damn, you as bad as her now," he said.

"Thank you," Patience replied.

Courtney shook his head. "I don't know what I'm going to do with y'all."

"Get us to Nicodemus," Corliss said.

Courtney rubbed his elbow as he looked into the sky.

"We ain't got that far to go," he said. "A day's walk, maybe two."

Patience expected to feel happy about the news. Instead, she was apprehensive. She was fulfilling papa's purpose and would finally be able to give Ms. Harriet his bois. But what would she do afterwards? Would she return to Trinidad? Or would she remain in Nicodemus? The second thought hadn't crossed her mind until that moment. Could she start a new life there?

She slept fitfully that night, hoping Papa would come to her and give her guidance. He didn't. They morning when she awoke, she half-expected him to enter her mind with words of encouragement or congratulations but neither occurred. A cold sensation caused her to shiver. Was he gone? Had he moved on without saying goodbye? The thought forced tears out of her eyes.

"You alright baby?"

Corliss walked toward her; her arms outstretched. Patience rushed to meet her, eager for her comforting hug. She was crying hard now.

"Calm down," Corliss said. "Tell me what's wrong."

"Papa's gone," she said. "He's gone."

Corliss held her tighter.

"It was bound to happen sooner or later," she said. "He stayed with you as long as he needed. Now that you're about to meet Ms. Harriet his work is done."

"But he didn't say goodbye!" Patience sobbed.

"He didn't? Well, that means you'll see him again."

They broke camp without breakfast, working their way from the tracks to the road leading to Nicodemus. The landscape was strange to Patience; miles and miles of rolling hills and grass. Herds of buffalo shared the expanse with sod house farms, the farmers halting their chores to observe the trio as they walked down the dirt road. Corliss hummed a tune and they all kept pace. Patience strained her eyes, looking for signs of the city and the end of her long journey but saw nothing.

The sun was directly overhead when she spotted figures in the distance. As they came closer the figures came into view, a large man leading three saddled horses. The man was dressed simply, blue worn coveralls over dingy long johns. In one hand he held the reins of the horses. The other hand gripped the handle of a sledgehammer that rested on his right shoulder.

"Is that him?" Corliss asked.

Courtney shaded his eyes from the noon-day sun.

"Looks like him. I don't know for sure. Never seen him before."

The man strolled toward them a bit closer then stopped, waiting for them to approach. They stopped a few feet away from him; the man grinned then tipped his hat.

"Howdy," he said. "I'm John Henry. Miss Tubman sent me to fetch y'all."

Courtney stepped forward then he and John shook hands.

"I'm Courtney Brimstone. These are my sisters, Corliss and Patience."

Corliss stepped forward and shook John Henry's hand.

"Pleased to meet you," she said. "I heard some stories about you."

"Do tell?" John said. "I hope they were good ones."

"Unbelievable, actually," Corliss said.

"Heard the same about y'all," John replied. "That's why I brought my hammer."

The three of them laughed, breaking the tension. John looked past Courtney and Corliss to Patience. Her throat dried up; when she spoke, her voice was weak like a kitten's mew.

"Hello, sir," she said.

"Ain't no need of that formal stuff," John said. "Glad you made it. Miss Tubman was real worried about you, but your daddy told her you was gonna be alright."

Patience's eyes went wide and her heart drummed.

"My Papa is here?" she asked.

John's face took on a sad expression.

"He ain't here like you're thinking," he said. "But Miss Tubman can see him just like you."

Patience shoulders slumped.

"Oh."

John glanced at the horses.

"I brought these for y'all. Miss Tubman figured y'all would be tired of walking."

"Thank you, Jesus!" Corliss exclaimed. She ran over and climbed on a black stallion. Courtney mounted the Appaloosa, which left the roan mare for Patience.

"Alrighty then," John said. "Let's get y'all home."

Patience settled into the saddle and took a deep breath. So Papa had left her to let Miss Tubman know they were coming. Who was this woman who summoned Papa to America and who could take his spirit from her as she pleased? Patience was not sure she would like her. Patience's life had been safe and simple, but because of Miss Tubman papa was dead and she was being pursued by some kind of monster.

"It's not her fault," Papa said.

"Papa!" she exclaimed out loud. "You're back!"

The others looked and her and smiled.

"Yes, I am," he said. *"Miss Tubman is not the reason for your woes. These are things that would have happened no matter where we were. The truth is that if it were not for Harriet, we both would be dead."*

"Courtney said we could still die," Patience replied. "He said Jedediah Green is very powerful."

"Courtney is right," papa said. *"But we have a better chance together. You'll understand once you meet Harriet the others."*

"There are others?"

"Yes. The ancestors were generous with their gifts. Some were never aware of them. They

lived and died never knowing what power they possessed. Others were lucky like us. We had elders that recognized our blessings and helped us develop them."

"But why give us such talents?" Patience said.

"To protect those we can," Papa said.

"There it is!" Corliss said, interrupting her conversation with Papa.

Rising over the horizon was a scattering of wooden buildings divided by dirt streets. Nicodemus was smaller than she imagined, yet there was an aura that extended from the town and drew her toward it. Relief washed over her; the journey was finally over. She would meet Miss Tubman, give her papa's bois then return to Trinidad.

"They're waiting for us in the saloon," John Henry said.

"We can't take Patience in a saloon," Corliss said. "It ain't proper."

"It's not that kind of place, not in Nicodemus," John said. "Miss Tubman wouldn't let that kind of going on happen here."

They rode down the main street. People nodded and waved to them, each going about their daily chores. The Negroes in this town seemed more relaxed than any she'd seen since she came to America. It reminded her of Trinidad, with the exception of the constant breeze and the smell of the ocean. John Henry led them to the saloon then tied their horses to the hitching post. He climbed the stairs as the three of them dismounted.

"Y'all come on in," he said. "Everyone's waiting."

Patience, Corliss and Courtney followed John through the swinging doors. A round table filled the center of the room, occupied by three people. There was a stern yet pretty woman dressed in a pinstripe blouse and walking skirt, outfit, a strange necklace gracing her neck. A man sat beside her, his clothing resembling a lawman's without the badge. A large moustache rested on his lips, a wide brim hat on his head. Beside him sat an aged woman, her head covered in a plain white wrap. The woman smiled as they approached the table, a welcoming smile on her face.

"Thank the Lord y'all made it," the woman said. "We're all here now and none too soon."

Patience walked around the table to the woman, her arms wrapped around the bois box.

"Miss Tubman?" she asked.

"Hello Patience," Miss Tubman said. "I've been waiting for you."

Patience gave the bois box a squeeze before extended it toward Miss Tubman.

"My Papa wanted me to give you this," she said, her voice shaking with emotion. "He would have given it to you himself, but . . . but . . ."

Patience lost her voice to grief. Her shoulders slumped as she began crying. Miss Tubman rose then shuffled to her and took her into a warm and surprisingly strong hug.

"It's alright now," she said. "Me and your papa had a long talk the other day. He told me to tell you that he will always be in your heart and your bois."

Patience opened the box then took the bois in her hands. The stick was warm and pleasant in her hands, causing her to smile.

"You are still with me, papa," she whispered.

Miss Tubman stood then hugged Corliss and Courtney.

"Thank y'all for bringing her," she said.

"Weren't no problem," Courtney said.

"I'm so proud to meet you," Corliss said. "So proud."

Corliss opened her fiddle case and took out the white object Missy had given to her.

"Missy told me to make sure you got this."

Sadness flushed Miss Tubman's face as she took the object.

"Missy was a good, strong woman," Miss Tubman said. "We'll put this to good use."

She put the cube in her dress pocket before shuffling over to stand between the man and woman sitting at the table.

"Y'all done met John, she said. "This here is Dorothy Wright, and this here is Bass Reeves."

"Glad to meet you," Dorothy said.

"Howdy," Bass said.

"Y'all come on now," Harriet said. "Y'all need to get some food in your bellies and get some rest."

Harriet looked at Dorothy.

"Dot, you and John get these folks straight. Me and the others got to get prepared.

"Prepared for what?" Patience asked.

Miss Harriet's face turned grim. "You didn't think ol' Jedediah was going to stop coming for y'all just because you came to Nicodemus, did you?"

"I hoped so," Patience replied.

"Jedediah has to be dealt with," Harriet said. "Ain't no running away from what he brings."

"What does he bring?"

"Balance."

Miss Harriet pointed over Patience's shoulder. She turned see a storm churning on the horizon, one like she'd never seen before. An eerie blue light flashed among its clouds. For a moment Patience thought she was observing one of the famous mid-west storms she'd heard about as far away as Trinidad. There was something different about this storm; the blue light didn't flash erratically like lighting was prone to do. It pulsed with the rhythm of a heartbeat.

"That's Jedediah," Miss Tubman said. "And he's coming to collect his due."

"Come on," Dorothy said. "Let's get some food on them bones."

"Begging your pardon, ma'am, I'd just as soon stay out here," Courtney said. "If Jedediah's coming I'd like to be the first to say hello."

"You ain't any good to me weak," Harriet fussed. "Now you get on and get you something to eat, you hear?"

Miss Harriet's voice took the tone of a mother scolding her child and Courtney responded like a disciplined child. He kicked the at the floor then pouted.

"Come on, little sister," Corliss said. "I kind of agree with Courtney, but I don't fancy dying on an empty stomach."

"You're supposed to be on my side," Courtney said.

"I'm on food's side," Corliss said. "Now come go with me and Patience. You need it as much as we do."

Courtney relented and the three of them followed Miss Dorothy. Patience pulled on Corliss's skirt to get her attention. Corliss responded with one of her comforting smiles.

"What is it, baby girl?"

"What did Miss Harriet mean by Jedediah collecting his due?"

There was a crack in Corliss's usually cool demeanor; one so short Patience almost missed it.

"Let's not worry about that right now," Corliss said. "Let's get that little belly full."

When they entered the restaurant, it was empty. Miss Dorothy didn't seem to notice; she ambled through the business as if nothing was amiss. They followed her through the servant's door and into the kitchen. It was empty of people yet filled with the various aromas of a large and tasty meal.

"Where is the staff?" Patience asked.

"Home," Dorothy replied. "Kansas is known for its storms. They're all probably gathering as much of their belongings as they can then heading for their storm basements."

Dorothy gathered up plates then began opening the simmering pots.

"Y'all go on back to the dining area. I'll fix y'all plates."

"You sure you'll be okay?" Courtney said. "I know my way around a kitchen."

"I'm fine," Dorothy said. "Now do what I'm telling you. The food with be out momentarily."

They returned to the dining area and picked a table near the kitchen exit. Dorothy came out fifteen minutes later with loaded plates. She served the trio then sat with them.

"You ain't eating," Corliss asked.

"No," Dorothy said. "I ate earlier. I hate fighting on an empty stomach."

"Will come to that?" Patience asked.

Miss Dorothy laughed "It will most definitely come to that."

Patience shuddered. She didn't want to fight, but she also didn't want to avoid this duty. Papa had come to America to stand with Miss Tubman and she would have to take his place. Corliss and Courtney gave her reassuring smiles as they ate, but it did nothing to allay her nervousness. She would love to hear Papa's voice, but he was silent. She looked about the room hoping to find something to distract her attention. Her eyes rested on Dorothy's necklace.

"That's a pretty necklace Miss Dorothy," she said.

Miss Dorothy touched the amber necklace then frowned.

"Pretty to look at," she said. "A burden to wear."

"That's Miss Dorothy's talisman," Corliss whispered. "She ain't too fond of it."

"No, I'm not," Dorothy said. "Y'all need anything else?"

"No ma'am," Courtney said.

"I'm going back to the saloon. Y'all come on when you're done. Don't tarry too long. We got work to do."

Dorothy strolled out the restaurant.

"She's not very friendly," Patience said.

"Miss Dorothy has been with Harriet longer than anyone," Courtney said. "She's done more than any of the others. This is a weight that can wear on a person's soul it they ain't prepared for it."

"Y'all quit talking and finish," Courtney said. "They waiting for us."

"You sure in a hurry to see Jedediah," Corliss teased. "I'm beginning to think you miss him."

"I'm ready to get this over with," Courtney replied. "That devil done caused too much pain for too long."

"Amen!" Corliss said.

They hurried through the meal then returned to the saloon, their eyes on the darkening skies. Everyone waited in the saloon at the table. The others nodded as they sat.

"This ain't no complicated plan," Miss Harriet said. "But it's going to take every last one of us doing the best they can. Bass, Dorothy, you two will take the lead. Your job is to clear a path. Corliss, I'm going to need you to play that fiddle of yours better than you ever have to slow them hounds and whatever else Jedediah is bringing with him. John, Courtney and I will handle Jedediah. God willing we're enough."

"What about me?" Patience asked.

"You'll be Corliss's bodyguard," Harriet said. "No matter how good Bass and Dorothy are at shooting, some of them hounds and things are bound to slip by. It's your job to make sure they don't get anywhere near Corliss. Can you do that?"

"Yes ma'am. I can."

"Good."

Thunder shook the building and Harriet grinned.

"Looks like Jedediah is calling us out. Let's not disappoint him."

Miss Harriet led them out of the saloon and into the street. Harriet gripped her bois tight, fighting the fear that threatened to overwhelm her.

"We are with you," she heard her Papa say. His voice pushed the fear away; she smiled as her confidence returned.

"I don't care what happens Papa," she said. "If I die today, I'll be with you and mama. That's not so bad."

"It's not bad at all, cheri," Papa said.

The sky churned black with swirling gray clouds. As the group emerged from the city building shapes could be seen advancing in the distance. Bass and Dorothy picked up their pace, moving ahead of the others. Bass took off his jacket and dropped it to the ground, exposing his revolvers. Dorothy loaded her Henri, the amber necklace taking on a faint glow. Corliss halted, removing her fiddle and bow from the worn case and bracing it against her chin. Patience stood in front of her, holding her bois in the guard position.

"You ready, little sister?" Corliss asked.

"Yes, big sister."

Courtney smiled at them both.

"This will only take a minute," he said.

"Courtney!" Miss Harriet called out.

"Coming Miss Tubman!"

Courtney ran to catch up with Miss Harriet and John Henry. He unsheathed his machetes as he reached them. John took his sledgehammer off his shoulder then cut a figure eight in the air before him. Miss Harriet shook her head.

"Boys always showing off," she said.

"When you going to transform?" John asked.

"As soon as I figure out what we need."

The shapes finally came into view. It was the hellhounds, hundreds of them, their paws tearing the ground.

"It's time you play that fiddle, gal," Harriet called out.

"Hold tight," Corliss said to Pauline. "This is going to be a bad one."

Corliss dragged her bow across the fiddle strings. Patience was used to the sound, but this song was more piercing. She struggled not to drop her bois and cover her ears. Whatever effect it had on her, the song was more devastating to the hellhound horde. The hounds fell over each other and careened in every direction. Bass and Dorothy moved in guns blazing. They killed the hounds by the dozens, Dorothy reloading the Henri in a flash, Bass firing round after round without pausing. Patience realized the revolvers were his talisman. Whatever came from the barrels of his guns were not bullets.

Dorothy and Bass were finishing off the last of the hounds when another wave attacked. These hounds were larger and were barely affected by Corliss's song. Bass and Dorothy stood shoulder to shoulder, shooting the second wave down, but these beasts needed more firepower to bring them down. They slipped by, but their success was short lived. John Henry batted the strays with his hammer, sending them back the way they came or smashing them into the dirt. Courtney sliced them in half with his machetes, a wide grin on his face. Miss Harriet did nothing. She continued to walk forward, oblivious to the carnage, her rheumy eyes focused on the center of the storm.

A hound survived the gauntlet and charged for Patience and Corliss. Patience took a quick glance at Corliss; her sister was caught up in her song, her eyes blank. Patience took a deep breath then ran toward the beast, her bois held high. Just as she was about to deliver a blow the hound leapt over her, landing on its paws and speeding toward Corliss. Patience spun about and ran after it. It was too fast; there was no way she would catch it before it reached Corliss.

"Corliss!" she shouted, but Corliss did not respond.

"Corliss!"

Her eyes watered as she realized she was about to see her sister die.

Patience threw the bois with all her strength. The stick flew from her hands then tangled itself with the hound's rear legs. The hound tumbled, rolling end over end until it skidded to a halt a few feet before Corliss. Patience scooped up the bois as she ran to the beast as it struggled to regain its paws.

"Hey!" she shouted. She gripped the bois with both hands together and swung with all her might as she neared the beast.

The beast turned into the bois. Blood and fangs flew from its mouth as its head twisted. Patience raised the bois then brought it down on the hound's head. Wood met bone and bone gave way with a sickening crunch. The hound collapsed onto its chest and died; its legs spread apart as if praying.

Another beast broke through. Patience charged for it, blocking the way between it and Corliss. This hound did not attempt to avoid her. It came up on Patience so quickly she didn't have time to prepare a blow. Instead, she stabbed the bois into the hound's maw and out of the back of its head. She drew her arm back but not fast enough; the hound's teeth furrowed the skin on her forearm and she grimaced. The wounds burned with its acrid saliva but she had no time to suffer. More hounds were making their way through, too many for her to handle. She braced herself for the onslaught, sure she was about to see mama and papa again. A sudden gust shoved her away from the hounds; she tried to move toward them and the wind pushed her to the ground.

"Don't move child," Miss Harriet's voice said. "I'll take care of this."

Harriet took Missy's cube from her pocket then slammed it to the ground. A burst of whiteness swallowed her; moments later the whiteness began to spin, escalating quickly into a small but intense whirlwind. It sucked the hounds into its center, the beasts howling in pain and shock as the twister spun faster and faster. The wind ended abruptly, flinging the hounds in every direction. The dust and grass cleared to reveal Miss Harriet standing alone.

"Got to get back to them boys before it's too late," Miss Harriet said. She ran toward

Jedediah's storm faster than Patience imaged her capable.

"Corliss is going to fine now," she called out. "Come with me, Patience!"

Patience followed Miss Harriett. The hounds still attacked but their numbers were diminishing. Dorothy and Bass shot a path open for them and they ran to the battle taking place only a few yards away. Patience saw Jedediah Green for the first time and she stopped running. He was tall as two Courtneys and heavily muscled like a Greek statue. His clothes gripped his massive body like a second skin; his eyes burned like a wildfire. John Henry swung his hammer as effortlessly as Patience handled her bois, but Jedediah dodged his blows with a gracefulness that belied his size. Courtney hacked at the giant as well, occasionally landing cuts that had no effect on Jedediah. The storm bringer grinned as he fought. Their mighty struggle seemed a game to him. He looked away from his attackers, his eyes finding Miss Harriet for a moment then focusing on Patience.

"There you are," he said, his voice ringing in her head. "We're all here now."

Jedediah caught John Henry's hammer with his left hand then punched the man in his chest, sending him sprawling into the mud. He swung the hammer without looking and hit Courtney in the stomach. Courtney dropped his machetes and curled around the hammer. He tried to clutch it but Jedediah shoved him away like an errant insect. Miss Harriet continued running toward Jedediah, her hands raised over her head. Patience ran after her.

Jedediah threw the hammer at Harriet. She dodged it, continuing to run at Jedediah. Patience watched as the hammer froze then streaked back toward Jedediah, its path taking it directly at Miss Harriet.

"Miss Harriet! Look out!" Patience shouted.

Miss Harriet spun about but she saw the hammer too late. It struck her head and she collapsed where she stood. Patience ran to Miss Harriet then stood over her. Jedediah caught the hammer then looked at Patience.

"That was easier than I imagined," he said.

He raised the hammer. Patience braced herself, her bois raised over her head. Before Jedediah could release the hammer, he was peppered with lead. Bass and Dorothy appeared on either side of her, shooting as fast as their weapons allowed.

"This ain't going to hold him," Bass shouted. "Somebody better get Miss Harriet on her feet before we all be having a meeting in Heaven!"

Patience dropped to her knees beside Miss Harriet. She lifted her head and shook her gently.

"Miss Harriet, Miss Harriet, please wake up," she whispered. "Please!"

A loud howling came from Jedediah. Patience turned to see Jedediah staggering, holding his left side. Courtney followed him, machetes his in his hands. Bass and Dorothy watched as well, their guns silent.

"Why aren't you shooting?" Patience yelled.

"Courtney's too close," Dorothy replied. "We might hit him."

Patience laid Miss Harriet's head down gently, jumped to her feet then ran toward Courtney and Jedediah.

"Ancestors," she whispered. "I need you."

The bois burned in her hands as the ancestors came forth, filling her with their power.

"Get back here!" Bass shouted.

Patience didn't listen. Jedediah didn't notice her until she was almost upon him. He turned toward her as she leaped and swung her bois, smashing it against his cheek so hard his head twisted. Before he could attack Courtney's machete sliced at his shoulder. Courtney and Patience performed a deadly dance around Jedediah, timing their attacks so that the demon could not retaliate. But Patience was tiring. Each blow was weaker than the next; each dodge was closer to disaster. Jedediah's storm was full upon them, obscuring her vision. She didn't see Jedediah's fist until it was too late. Her chest felt as if it was going to shatter, her bois flying from her hands. She struck the wet ground, rolling end over end until falling into a water-filled depression. Fluid filled her mouth and nose; she jerked upright gagging and coughing. Patience expected Jedediah to arrive any moment to finish her and without her bois there was no way she could stop him. But the attack did not come. Instead, she heard Courtney shouting her name through the maelstrom.

"Patience! Patience! God dammit girl I need you!"

Patience pulled herself out of the pool then tried to stand. Her left ankle cried out in pain and she almost fell backwards into the muddy pool again. She steadied herself on her good leg then hobbled toward Courtney's voice while seeking her bois through the downpour. She found her bois and hope jumped back into her heart. Papa's voice filled her head.

"Hurry! He's almost there!"

Patience hobbled faster. The ever-present warmth of the bois flowed from her palms to her ankle. The pain subsided as did her ankle and her hobble transformed into a run. Her feet splashed across the wet ground, mud caking the edges of her skirt. Hope faded as she neared Jedediah. Both Dorothy and Bass sprawled in the grass; she couldn't tell if they were dead or unconscious. She could hear Corliss's playing up ahead; at least she was still alive. Finally, she saw Courtney ahead of her, his machete sheaths bouncing off his back. She picked up her pace then caught him, running alongside him.

"We can't stop him," he said without looking at her. "Miss Harriett is having one of her seizures. You need to go to Corliss and tell her I said it's time to play that song."

"That song?" Patience said.

"Yes," he replied.

"How am I going to get past Jedediah?" she asked.

"He ain't paying no attention to us now. All he can see is Miss Harriett and Nicodemus. Now you get on and do as I told you!"

Patience ran on, her bois tight in her fists. She ran wide of the storm that was Jedediah, the rain slacking as she passed him. She could see the town in the distance, the residents huddled inside the wooden building and storm shelters braced for what they thought was another storm. But it was much worse. Standing between them and their destruction was Corliss. She'd put her fiddle away and stood legs wide, her machetes in her hands.

"Corliss!" Patience shouted. "Corliss!"

Corliss looked in her direction and an expression of relief washed over her face. Patience ran up to her then stopped for a moment to catch her breath.

"Where's Courtney?" Corliss asked.

"He's coming up behind Jedediah," Patience said. "He told me to tell you to play that song."

Corliss's eyes went wide. "He told you to tell me that?"

"Yes," Patience said.

Corliss closed her eyes for a moment. When she opened them they glistened. She sheathed her machetes then took out her fiddle. She pressed it against her shoulder this time.

"Goodbye brother," she whispered.

Her words puzzled Patience until she heard the tune. It was the same song Corliss played when Courtney made the power that destroyed the hellhounds. But it rained, which meant the only way he could use it against Jedediah was to deliver it himself.

"No!"

Patience ran toward the storm. If she could reach Jedediah before Courtney, she could stop him. She saw Courtney closing in on Jedediah, the demon's attention caught up by his immense storm. Courtney reached Jedediah then jumped on his back; Corliss struck a high-pitched shrill tone and Patience was engulfed by brightness. It swallowed her and lifted her off her feet, carrying her away like a feather in a whirlwind then dropping her onto the wet earth. She slid on her back for yards before stopping. The light subsided, taking its warmth with it. When she finally opened her eyes, she looked into a starlit sky giving way to the approaching dawn. She lay there as the numbness gave way to a rising tide of fatigue and pain. She groaned as she sat up then shook her head, her bois in her hand, pulsing warm like a heartbeat. Patience finally looked where she last saw Courtney and was stunned. A wide crater stretched out before her, mist rising from it like steam. She clambered to her feet the stumbled toward the edge.

"Courtney?" she called out.

When she reached the rim, she saw Corliss standing in the middle of the depression, fiddle in one hand, and bow in the other. Patience scrambled down the side of the crater, then trudged through the scorched mud and burned grass to her sister's side. She reached out and touched Corliss's hand. Corliss looked at her with teary eyes.

"He's gone," she said. "And he took Jedediah with him."

Patience moved closer to Corliss, wrapping her arms around her waist. She had lost Papa, so she knew how Corliss felt. There were no words that would take the pain away. All she could do was hold her and listen.

"Don't remember a day without him," Corliss said. "Jedediah brought us to life the same day. We were his twins, his favorites. Guess it was only right that one of us put him down."

They stood together for what seemed like hours. Finally, Corliss tapped her shoulder.

"Let's go, baby girl," she said. "We got to see if the others are alright."

They made their way toward the rim. As they came closer their cohorts appeared. Bass and Dorothy stood at the crater's edge, Dorothy cradling her Henri, Bass hands on his revolver grips. John Henry limped up, his hammer resting on his shoulder. Finally, Miss Harriett appeared, a serene look on her face. They climbed out of the pit and the others surrounded them, giving them praise and hugs.

"That was some fine work," John said.

"Never seen anything like it," Bass agreed.

"Nice," Dorothy commented.

Miss Harriett hugged both of them tight.

"I'm so sorry," she said. "I figured Jedediah had come for me and I was ready to pay the price to right the Balance. Looks like he came for one of his own."

"Is it over, Miss Tubman?" Patience asked.

"It ain't never over with Jedediah," Miss Harriett replied. "But we won't see him again, at least not in your lifetime."

Miss Harriett stepped away to regard them all.

"Y'all done good," she said. "The ancestors are proud of you. Now we need to get back to doing what we were sent here to do."

"And what is that, Miss Harriett?" Patience asked.

"Protect Nicodemus and serve our people," Miss Harriet replied.

They walked to Nicodemus, Dorothy and Bass leading the way.

TEN

It was the worst storm Nicodemus had ever seen. The town suffered extensive damage and lives were lost. Still, it wasn't as bad as it could have been. The people came out of hiding and immediately went to work. Buildings were repaired and family, relatives and friends were buried. After a few weeks life in Nicodemus was routine again, if not back to normal.

Patience and Corliss stood before Miss Harriett in her parlor, holding hands. Courtney's death had forged them as sisters and they had spent every moment after the battle together. Miss Harriett stirred the cup of tea in her hand before taking a sip. She nodded then placed the cup on her table before looking into Patience's weary eyes.

"You suffered a lot on this journey," she said. "I'm sorry it had to be this way, but every special person needs a forging to find out what they are. I'd say you done well."

Patience wanted to be proud, but Papa's and Courtney's passings wouldn't allow her to be. All she felt was sadness.

"Now that we're settled, I called y'all here to ask you what you planned on doing. Of course, you're welcomed to stay here in Nicodemus. But the choice is up to you."

"I want to go home," Patience blurted. "I want to go back to Trinidad. Papa came to bring you his bois, and now you have it."

"That's true," Miss Harriett replied. She picked up the box containing the talisman then extended to Patience.

"Take it," she said. "Your Papa never intended to stay here. This is your heritage. All I ask is if I need you again, you'll come if I call."

Patience took the bois then cradled it against her chest. Its warmth soothed her and brought a smile to her face.

"I will," she said.

"In the meantime, you watch over your people in Trinidad like we do here in Nicodemus," Miss Harriett said. "You've been given a gift. Use it with purpose."

"I shall," Patience replied.

"And what about you, Corliss?" Miss Harriett asked. "Will you be staying with us?"

"No ma'am," Corliss said. "I've always been one of a pair and as hospitable everyone is in Nicodemus, I got to stay with family."

Corliss grasped Patience's hand and Patience smiled. She looked up at her big sister.

"You'll love Trinidad," she said.

"I better," Corliss replied.

"Then it's settled," Miss Harriett said. "When do y'all plan on leaving?"

"Today," Patience said. "We have a long walk ahead."

"Won't be no walking," Miss Harriett replied. "I'll have John fix y'all up a wagon with two good mules and plenty of supplies. We'll also give you a few dollars for more when you run dry."

Miss Harriett stood then hugged them both. Patience never knew her mother's touch, but she imagined it would feel like this.

"Goodbye to you both and good travels."

Apparently, Miss Harriett had figured their plans, for when they exited her home John was waiting with the wagon. He strolled up to them then hugged them.

"I'm sorry I didn't get to know y'all better, and I'm sad we met under difficult circumstances," he said.

The women climbed into the wagon, Corliss taking the reins.

"Y'all be safe now, and God bless you."

"We will," Patience replied. "And He will."

Patience snapped the reins and they were on their way. They passed the schoolhouse where Miss Dorothy worked. The stern woman emerged and waved them goodbye. As they reached the outskirts of town Bass Reeves stepped outside of the Marshall's office and tipped his hat to them. Patience looked ahead into the sea of grass and imagined the blue waters surrounding her home. She would see them again soon. She squeezed the bois box.

"We're going home Papa," she whispered. "We're going home."

-End-

ABOUT THE AUTHOR

Milton Davis is an award winning Black Speculative fiction writer and owner of MVmedia, LLC, a publishing company specializing in Science Fiction and Fantasy based on African/African Diaspora history, culture and traditions. Milton is the author of twenty-one novels and short story collection and editor/coeditor of tent anthologies. His short stories have appeared in a number of anthologies and magazines, most notably Black Panther: Tales of Wakanda, Obsidian Literature and Arts in the African Diaspora and Tales from the Magician's Skull. Milton's story 'The Swarm' was nominated for the 2017 British Science Fiction Association Award for Short Fiction and his story, Carnival, was nominated for the 2020 British Science Fiction Association Award for Short Fiction. Milton Davis can be found at www.miltonjdavis.com.

Looking for more exciting Steamfunk Stories? Check out these titles from MVmedia!

www.mvmediaatl.com

Steamfunk!
Edited by Milton J. Davis and Balogun Ojetade

A witch, more machine than human, judges the character of the wicked and hands out justice in a ravaged Chicago. John Henry wields his mighty hammers in a war against machines and the undead. Frederick Douglass and Harriet Tubman rule a country of freed slaves that rivals – and often bests – England and France in power and technology. You will find all this – and much more – between the pages of Steamfunk, an anthology of incredible stories by some of today's greatest authors of Science Fiction, Fantasy and Steamfunk – African and African American-inspired Steampunk.

From Here to Tumbuktu
By Milton J. Davis

The year is 1870. As the young country of Freedonia prepares to celebrate fifty years of existence, a young bounty hunter by the name of Zeke Culpepper is hired by a wealthy businessman to find a valuable book. In the kingdom of Mali on the continent of Africa, veteran warrior Famara Keita has been assigned to find that same book and bring it back to its rightful owner. And in the newly formed nation of Germany, an ambitious Prussian officer seeks the book as well for its secrets that could make Germany the most powerful nation in the world. The result is an action adventure like no other!

La Rosa de Matanzas
(The Rose of Mtanzas)
By Milton J. Davis

For ten years Pauline Rose has lived a new life in Freedonia. As her relationship with bounty hunter Zeke Culpepper begins to grow, her past comes back to haunt her. She finds herself in the custody of General Phillipe Gonzales on her way back to Cuba to stand trial for crimes committed . . . as a revolutionary fighter!
When Pauline turns up missing, Zeke swings into action, seeking his woman and the reason she was taken. The result is an adventure bursting with intrigue and revelation as Zeke learns the secret of La Rosa de Matanzas!

Rite of Passage
By Milton J. Davis

The Rite of Passage stories are exciting Steamfunk tales light on the steam yet heavy on history and the supernatural. They take place during and after Reconstruction and follow a group of talented individuals led by Harriet Tubman. These special people converge on the town of Nicodemus, Kansas, protecting its inhabitants from the inequalities of the North and the evil shadow of Jim Crow.

Masquerade
By
Milton J. Davis

In the city of Barakoa, the mask is everything. It signifies your rank, your personality, your past, present and future. Jeremy Pepperdine waited for all these things to be bestowed upon him on his sixteenth birthday. But after a tragic event Jeremy finds himself, abandoned, alone . . . and maskless. How does a person survive in a world where the most important item of the society is denied to him?